Silent Snow

Tales from Ancient Ieda 01

Sarah Thomie

ISBN-13: 978-1-955627-00-9

Cover design by: Clarissa Kezen
(http://ckbookcoverdesigns.com/)

Printed in the United States of America

This book is dedicated to:
Ryan
Big Z
Little Z
Baby Z
Asha the Void
Cali the Orange

TW: Sexual assault, birth trauma mentioned, death, dark

70k words

Good Morning, love!

Thank you for purchasing Silent Snow!

This is S. Thomie's debut story of the world of Ieda.

Those written as Ancient Ieda are medieval fantasy, while Modern Ieda is more urban fantasy.

Chapter 01

"Run!" a male screamed. My fear and desperation overrode the fatigue or exhaustion. I had to get away from the burning buildings before the King's Guard showed up to investigate the fire growing behind me.

Snow Cat rose in me, asking if I needed her help. I gave myself to the spirit, allowing her to take over my movements. My energy renewed. As I blinked, a shade of pale blue tinted my line of sight. The Snow Cat was in control, and my body moved of its own volition.

I ran through the woods, my feet carrying me through a mess of trees and bushes. I leapt over a fallen log, then splashed in the cold water waiting on the other side. Ashes clung to my skin; the smell of smoke followed me. When I found a clearing, I slowed and debated whether to keep to the forest or take the chance through the meadow. Night was coming, so I thought the darkness would hide me, even in the open spaces. So, I ran through the clearing, reaching the forest on the other side.

I do not know how long I ran, but my body slowed, unable to keep up the break-neck pace. There was a small fire ahead of me as the cold, night air cooled the hot sweat on my skin. I shivered and slid to a stop to see who owned the flames.

A large Wood Elf dressed in leathers walked back toward his camp. His dark brown skin and black hair glistened in the flickering light. He stood near his fire, taller than me by over a foot. His thick arms muscles hinted at the rest of his stature. His cloak caught my attention: a wolf pelt that looked warmer than the tatters of clothes I wore.

The man did not know what hit him when I tackled him from behind, plunging him face first to the ground. I made a grab for the wolf pelt, but he swung his arm back, catching me in the cheek.

I threw myself off him. The coppery taste of blood filled my mouth.

He rolled onto his back, then stood up. "A City Elf?"

I crouched, waiting to pounce again. We circled each other, his hands in front of him, while I looked for a weak spot. When I thought I found one, I launched myself at him.

He feigned his weakness, catching me by my upper arms. He then turned and slammed my back into the nearest tree. I tried to kick him, but he smashed me into the tree again, knocking the breath from my lungs. I gasped for air, trying to get away from him. He held onto my arms, bruising my pale skin with the force of his strength. The Snow Cat's rage erupted within me. I kicked him, my heel connected with his thigh, after he turned his body at the last second to prevent me from nailing him in the sensitive areas. He dropped me, backing away.

If I could not find a way to stay warm, then I was going to die. Both the Snow Cat and I knew it, so there was no chance of walking away without the pelt. After I landed on all fours, I launched myself at him again. He grabbed me, that pulled the two of us to the ground. The Elf used his feet to kick me over his head, and I crashed into a rock behind him. Tasting more blood in my mouth, I begged my body to get up, but my body refused. I slipped in the cold dirt, watching as he came closer. I tried to fight back, but darkness closed around me, my vision fading.

Chapter 02

I woke up in the morning light to the sound of cackling fire, my vision cleared of the Snow Cat's blue tint. I tried to move, but my hands and feet were bound. The leather shirt and pants under the soft wolf pelt warmed me. The Snow Cat was too tired to help me, so I was on my own.

"If you are planning on attacking me again, you should reconsider," the large Wood Elf said in the common language from nearby. "But if you are willing to play nice, I might even share my food with you."

I did not say anything, even if I could.

He walked over and helped sit me up, leaning on the log he sat on. "Are you going to be a good City Elf?" he asked.

I nodded to him, a tinge of excitement for warm food filled my aching bones.

He untied my wrists but kept my ankles bound. He handed me a wooden bowl with what looked like soup in it and sipped from it. The hot soup warmed me from the inside. I looked to the large Elf who just kept an eye on me, waiting to see if I would attack him again.

"What is a City Elf doing so far away from civilization?" he asked.

Using my fingers, I mimed running.

He just looked at me. "Too good to talk to a Wood Elf?" he spat.

I shook my head again, trying to stop him from thinking the wrong thing.

"You could at least tell me your name," he growled.

I blinked. He knew I was a City Elf, but did he not realize that none of us had names? I moved the wolf pelt and the sleeve of the leather shirt he put on me while I was unconscious. I showed him the brand on my wrist; the numbers 13-87-22 had been burned into my skin.

He ran his thumb over the brand, and I could almost see his anger rising.

I tried to pull my wrist back, but he refused to let go.

"You do not even have a name..." His dark eyes flashed at me. "Can you even speak?"

I shook my head, as he dropped my wrist. I wished I could have explained why, but without paper, I would not be able to write it down for him. Even if I used my hands to speak, I was not sure he would have understood the gestures.

"Where were you going when you attacked me? Your clothes were destroyed, so you must have been through something terrible. And what about the ash on your skin?" He looked at the ground, deep in thought. "I am guessing you were running from a fire."

I shrugged, at the first question. I had nowhere to run to, just away from. I nodded at his guess that I had been running for a while and about the fire.

He seemed hesitant before he said, "I need to bring you to the Elder. He will know what to do with you."

I waved my hands in front of me, hoping he would understand not to take me with him.

"You do not have a choice. Either you come with me, or I will leave you here to freeze."

I glared at the ground. He would realize how much of a curse I was to be around sooner rather than later.

"I will get the camp cleaned up, then I will release your ankles. If you try to attack me, I will leave you behind. Considering that the only reason you are warm is because of my good graces, you should think about your actions."

I showed him a rude hand gesture, and by the way he chuckled, he knew what I meant.

He broke down his camp around me: collapsing the small tent, dowsing the fire, and cleaning the pot and bowl he used. He stuffed them into his pack. He untied my ankles and helped me stand.

I stepped away from him but did not try to run. He would learn that I was cursed, so I wanted to keep the warm clothes on as long as possible.

"It is a day and a half walk back to the village. Do you feel up to it?"

I shrugged, not sure whether I could or not.

He led us through the forest, following game trails as they wove through the trees. He must have been a foot and a half taller than me, but he did not take his full gigantic steps, so I could keep up. He kept asking me questions, and I tried to answer what I could. He then asked me something I was not expecting, "Why were your eyes blue last night, but green today?"

I tilted my head to the side, trying to figure out how to answer that. I mimed that it was snowing, followed by a cat's claw, then as a ghost, as you would charade during fireside terror tales, finally pointing to my heart with my thumb.

It took him a second to understand, but he caught on. "You have a Snow Cat spirit within you?"

I smiled and nodded.

We fell into an easy silence as we moved through the forest. We stopped a few times to rest and eat and, again, when we saw a beautiful vista. I had never been outside a city before unless it was in a covered travel cage as my enslavers moved me from place to place. I was surprised that he allowed me the freedom to stop and stare as we hiked.

As nightfall came upon us, he pulled his pack off his shoulders and set up camp next to a river. "If we follow this river, we will reach the village by nightfall tomorrow."

I gazed at the clear, running water from a rock above the deep water. I leaned over it to try to see the smooth pretty stones under the water.

"Be careful," he warned. "That rock does not look stable."

I heeded his warning and tried to slide back to the solid ground. The rock slid forward, and I lost my footing. With a loud splash, I fell into the deep, cold river. I fell beneath the waterline, not able to swim above it. There was a loud splash near me as the Wood Elf dove into the water after me. He grabbed my wrist and swam the two of us back to the shore. He had me hold onto a bunch of roots while he climbed out of the water. He then grabbed me under my arms and pulled me onto the bank of the river.

He guided us back to the camp, where he had a fire built.

I shook in the wet clothes and cold, night air.

"Take your clothes off."

I wondered how I could tell him to go to the Abyss, until I saw that he was removing his own clothes as well. I turned away from him and undressed.

He grabbed the clothes from me and hung them on a branch above the fire to dry. He wrapped a blanket around me and pulled me closer to the fire.

I shivered, while he made his soup and handed me the bowl of it. I sipped on it, hoping it would get rid of the chill I felt.

After we finished eating, he grabbed me and tossed me in the tent. He shoved me under more blankets and crawled into the tent next to me. "Do not move," he said as he wrapped his arms and legs around me. He radiated body heat, and I stopped shivering. Soon, the day's walk and his heat drew me to the lull of sleep.

Chapter 03

I woke up warm and comfortable, until I saw the shadow above me.

"Lookie here, boys. We found ourselves a couple of love birds cuddling for warmth," the gravelly voice said from the shadows. It was another Wood Elf, and from the glares from my companion, they were not a part of his Clan. The new Elf bent down and grabbed me, pulling me to my feet. "Oooh. She is a City Elf. Look at her scars, she must be a bad girl." He smiled at two other Wood Elves with him. He grabbed my chin to meet his eyes. "Just how bad can you be, City Elf?"

Part of me debated if biting him in the nose would make the situation too much worse.

"Let her go," my travelling companion growled from where he sat up beside me.

"Do not move, unless you want my friends' arrow to go through you." He looked to the two other Elves as they knocked their bows, aiming at my traveling companion. The enemy looked at me and said, "We just want to play with your friend here. If she is a good girl, we will just rob you. If she is not, or if you try to attack us, we will kill you." He grabbed my hair. "Never seen silver hair on an Elf before."

"Boss?" one of the others asked. "He looks like the Moon Clan's enforcer."

The boss threw me to the third Elf, as he bent down to inspect my companion's face. "I believe you are right. We caught Howling Wolf with his pants down." The stranger laughed as he stood back up.

I looked at the Wood Elf in the tent. Even the City Elves knew of the viciousness of the Moon Clan and their Enforcer. No wonder the Snow Cat could not defeat him.

The leader looked between the two of us and said, "Did not know who you were getting into bed with, did you, girly?"

The Snow Cat rose in me, turning my vision with her blue eyes. The leader watched while I changed, subtle, but enough for him to know that something was wrong. I looked to my companion, appraising him.

"What the hell is this?" The leader grabbed me again.

I smiled, caressing the skin of the leader's chest with my fingertips. He shuddered under my touch, before he took a tiny step back, giving me the chance to grab the knife from his belt.

Then, I threw it in a smooth motion, where it slammed into the arm of the other Elf.

He dropped his bow, screaming in pain.

Rage filled the leader's face as I backed closer to the second archer. "Grab her!" he yelled at the other Elf holding his bow on Howling Wolf. The second archer dropped his bow too, grabbed my upper arms, and pulled me closer to his body.

I slammed my heel into his knee, forcing it backward.

He let me go, just as Howling Wolf slammed his elbow into the leader's face. The three Elves were yelling in pain and bleeding on the ground.

Howling Wolf grabbed the rope and tied them to the nearest tree.

Once they were subdued, I blinked, my vision back to mine. He threw me the dried clothes from above the fire, and I put them on, while he dressed. We broke camp down.

The leader screamed at us, "What the Seven Hells is she? She's not a normal City Elf!"

I shrugged, letting Howling Wolf answer, "She is the newest member of the Moon Clan. So, I suggest that if you get out of that, you warn your Clan that she could easily defeat you, even without the help of the rest of our Clan."

We left them there, walking next to the river, continuing toward the village. Once we were far enough from them, I stopped. I did not know how to ask it, but he must have read my face.

"I will have to talk to the Elder, but I doubt he will disagree with me after he sees you fight." He then hesitated before asking, "How are you so scarred? I did not get a good look when I changed you the first night and then again last night; I was more worried about hypothermia than seeing your skin."

I took a deep breath and let it out. I mimed someone with a whip.

"Their leader said that it is because you were bad. Is it because you fought against the humans that held you?"

I nodded, but when I saw the sadness in his eyes, I wondered if I should have kept the scars hidden.

"Let us get to the village." He settled whatever was on his mind.

I followed him, both of us lost in our thoughts. I was trying to reconcile what I had heard about Howling Wolf and about the Wood Elf who chose to spare my life after I attacked him. The Wood Elves were used by the humans to threaten City Elves. They told us that if we escaped, the Wood Elves would find us, and if our lives were not cut short, then it would be worse than what the humans did to us.

"We are here." He broke the spell of silence over us.

I looked to see a modest village of circular wooden huts. In the center of the village was the largest building. I could hear voices, laughing, talking, some singing. I stopped; the fear of the stories I was told by the humans prevented me from taking another step. It was one thing to travel with a Wood Elf; it was something entirely different to be surrounded by them. I took an involuntary step back, but Howling Wolf grabbed my hand.

"It is all right."

A beautiful, tall woman ran toward us. She wore a thick leather dress that flitted in the wind. Her long black hair trailed behind her the closer she came.

I hid behind Howling Wolf, thinking better the Wood Elf you know versus an unknown one.

"Wolf!"

"Sparrow!" He hugged her, and I wondered if they were a couple.

She spotted me and let him go. "Who is this?" She leaned down, her eyes more curious than anything else.

He pulled me around to his front, the top of my head coming up to his chest.

She leaned in, and I shrank away, trying to push myself through him. "Hello." She smiled at me, before looking back at Howling Wolf. "Where did you find a City Elf?"

"She found me," he admitted. "She was freezing and tried to steal my wolf pelt for warmth. She attacked me, and after I beat her, I decided that the Elder should see her to decide what to do."

She looked from him to me, then back to him. "She attacked you? She is like five foot nothing."

"Almost beat me, too." His jaw shifted into a grin.

That is not how I remembered that fight; I was pretty sure he beat me easily.

She looked back at me. "What is your name, City Elf?" I showed her my brand, and she tilted her head. "What is this?"

"City Elves don't get names, since they are considered property," an older, male voice answered her from behind her. The older man stepped into my view, and I could almost feel the respect that he commanded. His dark tan skin was wrinkling, and his dark eyes held no warmth toward me.

The Snow Cat growled from her den within me when we noticed the Snow Cat pelt around his neck and back.

He looked to Howling Wolf and asked, "What is the meaning of this?"

"Honorable Elder, I believe that she could be of use to our Clan," Howling Wolf answered. "I have seen her fight, so I believe that she can be useful to us."

The Elder laid his cold gaze onto me. "It is not like you to pick up strays. She can stay the night, but I want her gone by tomorrow night."

I almost sighed in relief. If I did not stay, then my curse would not harm anyone here.

Howling Wolf argued, "But Elder—"

"You dare talk back to me?" the Elder's voice edged on deadly. "This creature is cursed, and she will only bring ruin to the Clan if she stays."

I nodded.

He gestured to me. "Even she understands that she does not belong here."

Howling Wolf's chest fell. "May Grandfather see her? She cannot talk, and if she could, it would at least help her continue on her journey."

"You may." The Elder gave his permission as he left us.

Sparrow looked at Howling Wolf and I. "Brother, I have never heard you go against the Elder before. Why would you start now?" She gave me an appraising look.

"The way she acts, she has never been outside city walls, so I am worried. But I have seen her fight, so I worry if she is taken on by another Clan, that she could be used against us." He grabbed my shoulder and said, "Let us go see Grandfather." He then led me through the village Wood Elves stopped what they were doing to stare, then whispered to the closest Elf to them.

I kept my eyes to the ground, trying to not feel like an abomination. We reached the large building in the center of the village.

Sparrow opened the door. "Grandfather! Howling Wolf has something he wants to show you!" Her voice carried.

A man who looked to be the same age as the Elder came from a side room. He saw me and stopped "Is this...?"

Howling Wolf walked me over to the older man. "Grandfather, she needs your help."

I stepped toward the older man, feeling comfort radiating from him. He reminded me of the city Healer, so I wondered if

Wood Elves had the same kind of person. "So, she is the one the whole village is buzzing about." He smiled. "It is all right, City Elf. I will not hurt you."

I trusted him at his word. I showed him my wrist, letting him read the brand.

"13-87-22, what brings you to our village, besides my grandson?"

I mimed that I could not speak.

"Her voice is gone, and I was hoping there would be something you could do to help her. The Elder will not let her stay, so if she is to leave, it would be best if she could talk," Howling Wolf explained.

"13-87-22, come with me." The older man held my elbow in his hand as he led me to a larger interior room. An inferno blazed in the center of the room, and it reminded me of where I had just escaped.

I froze, unable to take another step closer to the raging fire. I did not see the room or the Wood Elves anymore, instead, I saw the city I ran from burning.

The older man came between the large fire and me. "It is all right, City Elf."

I shook my head, taking a step back. It was not okay, but I could not explain to them how it was not all right.

He looked at Howling Wolf, concern written on his face. "Have you seen her do this before?"

Howling Wolf shook his head. "No, I have not. She has been near fire for the past two nights, so I do not know where this is coming fr—" He looked at the ground, touching his chin with a hooked index finger. "But when she found me, she was covered in ash. So much of it, that her skin and hair was dark grey. I did not know she had silver hair until she fell in the river, and it dried."

"Maybe it was because you built small fires instead of a larger one like this," Sparrow mumbled.

I looked at her, nodding. I swallowed hard, trying to push the terror down.

"What kind of a fire did she run from that would cause her to be completely covered in ash?" She thought out loud.

The older man turned me away from the fire, so that I was looking at Howling Wolf. "Keep looking at him. I am going to cut your finger and use the blood to see what I can do to help your voice."

I nodded, not taking my eyes from Howling Wolf's own. I felt a prick of pain as the knife cut my finger. The blood burned, and I thought I was going to throw up, the memory of the smell attacking me.

Howling Wolf pulled me closer to him. "She looks sick."

I nodded, holding my hand in front of my mouth. Sparrow handed me some water, and I took sips, hoping to keep my stomach from rebelling. They were watching something behind me, and I could see the reflection of the fire in their eyes. I turned to face it, needing to see what they saw.

Images rose into the smoke, showing the three of them when and how my voice was stolen. They watched the City Elf Seller whip me for disobeying his commands. He gave an evil smile, as he used magic to rip my voice away from me, transferring it into a silver ball on a chain. He put the chain around his neck, a trophy. The images in the smoke disappeared, leaving only the blaze's regular smoke.

They then led me to a smaller room away from the flames, while they discussed what they saw. The older man told his grandson, "Since her voice was stolen with magic, the only way to return it is by magic. There is nothing I can do without the ball with her voice in it." He looked at me. "I will talk to the Elder about this and see if he is willing to extend your stay a little bit longer. If he does, you will have to work just as hard as the people who live here. Are you able and willing?"

I nodded to the older man.

"With winter coming, the Elder might allow you to stay until after planting season. We could always use more hands in harvesting the winter fruits." That decided, he looked to his grandchildren. "I assume she will be staying close to you two?"

"I have room for her." Sparrow smiled at the older man, then to me. "Since she is wearing Howling Wolf's clothes, I will let her borrow some of mine." She grabbed my tangled hair and let it fall back down. "I also want to play with her hair, since it feels different than mine."

"I need to give my full report to the Elder. Should I wait until after you talk with him?" Howling Wolf asked his grandfather.

"Do your report first. I have a feeling that he and I will be talking for most of the night." He smiled to me. "Good night, 13-87-22."

I bowed my head respectfully to him.

"Off to bed, you two." He practically pushed Sparrow and I out the door.

Sparrow walked me to her circle house. She opened the door, shoved me inside and into a chair.

I fell into it, as I felt the Snow Cat waiting at the edge to help me.

Sparrow smiled, "So, what are your intentions with my brother? You somehow got my heartless and cold brother to have emotions." She put her hands on the chair's arms, leaning in. Our noses almost touched, and I wondered if she knew how close to my teeth she was. "Are you planning on getting into his heart then ripping it out? Or are you planning on getting into his pants to see if you could get our family's legacy? Were you sent by a rival Clan to kill him in his sleep?"

What was she talking about? My intentions with her brother were to steal his Wolf pelt to get warm, then to go somewhere where I could not hurt anyone else. I shook my head to all her accusations. She must have seen my confusion because she backed away.

"Howling Wolf is the strongest male in the Clan, but he's also clueless on the wiles of women that want to use him. I just wanted to make sure that you weren't planning on harming him. Take this as a warning to stay away from him."

I wondered what happened to set her teeth on edge around women near Howling Wolf.

I looked around her small house. There was a bed off to one side, a small kitchen area on the opposite wall, next to a water closet. There was a fireplace near the bed, and the table with two chairs, where I sat. It was a warm and comfortable room, better than the stone walls of the people who owned me. It was a lot better than the shanties that other City Elves lived in.

"Now, take off his clothes, so we can work on the rat's nest you call hair."

I did as she commanded, since she was scary in her own right.

Despite seeing the memory, she sucked in a breath when she saw the extent of the scarring. "The humans did that to you?" She did not hide the anger in her voice. "Why would you allow them to do that to you? Why did you not fight them off?"

I realized that she did not understand that fighting always made the punishments worse.

How could I explain to this strong warrior of a woman that you did not fight the humans who owned you unless you had nothing to lose? I fought for others, which is why I had more scars than many other City Elves. The humans would not kill me, because my silver hair was a prize among slaves, so I often took the punishment of my fellow slaves.

Thankfully, Sparrow dropped it as she sat me back in the chair. She brushed my long, silver hair, drawing the knots and tangles out of it. She was gentle as she could be as she worked. Once she got all the tangles out, she braided it to keep the fine hairs contained. There was a knock on the door, and she answered it.

A woman's voice drifted in from outside, "The Elder asked us to bring the silver-haired City Elf these clothes and some food."

I stood up and walked to the door, not caring that they saw my scars. I grabbed the clothes from them and dipped my head as a thank you.

The three women stared at me, taking in everything from my pale skin, moonlight silver hair, and the thousands of scars that adorned my skin.

"It is not polite to stare." She looked at me. "Stop showing off the goods to everyone. City Elves might understand your scars, but we do not, so it is not polite to throw it into people's faces."

"Sparrow, do you think they are all covered like she is? I mean, those must have taken decades to accumulate."

I shook my head at her first question but nodded at her second one.

The woman looked at me. "Can you speak?"

I shook my head, and the looks of pity crossed their faces.

She looked back to Sparrow, her voice lightening. "So, we heard that your brother found her?"

"That is correct." Her voice unsure of why they would ask.

"Did you warn her away from him?" The women smiled.

I nodded yet again.

They just laughed, as she closed the door in their faces.

"Get dressed," she grumbled as she got ready for bed.

I unfolded the clothes to find leather pants and a shirt, smaller versions of what Howling Wolf wore, along with underwear and something to bind my chest. The final piece of fabric looked like the linen that Sparrow changed into, so I guessed it was a night dress. I put it on and set the rest of the clothes on the table. I looked around to see where I would sleep, deciding that the rug in front of the fire would be comfortable enough.

"What are you doing?" she asked as I sat down.

29

I mimed sleeping, and she sighed.

"The bed is big enough for the both of us."

I looked at the bed, then her, then stood up. I pushed down on the bed, feeling its softness. It was softer than anything I was ever allowed to touch outside of my normal duties.

"Get in, so we can sleep."

I climbed under the covers next to her and felt tears filling my vision. I sniffled as I used my arm to wipe away the free-falling water droplets.

"Are you crying?" She sat up and stared at me. Since she already saw, I did not lie to her. "Have you ever slept in a bed before?"

I shook my head. She growled when she wiped away my tears with the blanket, "Try to get some sleep." She laid back down, and I let the exhaustion from the last few days pull me to a dreamless sleep.

Chapter 04

Sparrow and the other women of the Clan showed me their day-to-day work. I helped wherever I could, hoping the Elder would allow me to stay after winter was over. The Wood Elves were nothing like what we were warned against. I knew they could kill if needed, but it was not the joyful slaughter that I had been taught. Howling Wolf made me a wooden whistle to use if I needed anything. We came up with a system that differentiated between needing a smidge of help with something versus an emergency.

He and the other men went on different missions every day, but they were back by nightfall. I guessed they were scouting for enemies to protect the Clan. I noticed that he wore black when the other warriors wore brown, which fit his status as their Enforcer.

At night, he would work with me with weapons, building up what the Snow Cat could use. As we sparred, she danced through his movements, watching and learning. He kept the practices a secret, worried what the Clan would think about teaching an outsider. Sparrow was the only one who knew, after she had followed us one day, thinking we were having a lover's triste or something like that. I became more confident with the spear than with the bow, but I had the most familiarity with the dagger, since all City Elves learned knife work in secret during short stints of time where we were not closely being watched by the humans. We shared our different techniques in honor of our myth of The Reckoning, a spirit that rose from the ashes of a wildfire to save our people. Wolf made me a sheath for a dagger that he traded a pelt for. It was very basic, but it was perfectly balanced.

One cold winter afternoon, a few months after arriving at the village, the women gossiped about Howling Wolf and how Sparrow kept warning potential suitors off. They asked me if I thought he was handsome. I nodded, and they pounced.

"What do you find to be his best feature?" The women talked about his eyes, his hair, his rippling muscles, but none of those is what made him handsome for me.

Objectively, I understood and agreed with the women. I did not say it, but I liked the fact that he danced with the Snow Cat, taught me how to fight better, and most of all, the pure look of joy and excitement on his face when I threw him into the dirt using a techniques he taught me. Those times were when I could see what the women were saying.

Two boys screamed from the village. I dropped the basket I was holding and took off towards the sound. The Snow Cat took over, spurred by the screams of younglings. I heard other shouts, as the large brown bear chased the boys into and through the village. A spear leaned against the wall, and I grabbed it then followed the bear and boys. The children fled into a dead-end area in their panic.

The bear stopped running; its prey cornered. I slid to a stop between the bear and the boys. I whistled over my shoulder for them to get down. They did as I commanded, ducking low to the ground.

The bear roared. I grabbed the dagger from its sheath, and stared at the creature, my blue tinted vision waiting to see what it would do. It lunged at me, but I moved to the side, slicing its skin. My goal was to anger it since that was the best way to keep its attention on me. The bear foamed at the mouth, and I wondered if that was normal. It lashed out, but I dodged its wild slash. I kept its attention on me, as I led it out of the village. The women stared as I kept attacking the bear to draw it away from the other Elves.

A loud whistle called some of the men back to the village. The bear turned toward the sound, but I caught its attention again with a slash to its wrist. Once we reached the forest, I hoped the bear would leave, but it attacked me. Its long claws dug into my right forearm and blood dropped down my skin. I dropped the dagger; pain numbed that arm.

The Snow Cat did not feel the pain, only acknowledging that I could not hold anything with that hand. She lunged, using my body to attack the bear. I jammed the spear's sharp point into the bear's throat, through the soft palate, and into the base of its skull. It tried to rip the spear out, but its weight pushed the spear into the ground, sending the point further into its brain. The bear fell over, and I pulled the spear from its throat. The Snow Cat retreated into her den within me.

I blinked, my vision me own again, and looked at the dying bear. I cried as I fell to my knees in front of the animal. I grabbed the dagger from the dirt, using my non-dominant hand. Then I set the bear's head in my lap and used the dagger to slash its throat, ensuring the end of its misery. I tried to apologize to the animal, but I knew it would not hear me, even if it was still alive. I stroked the bear's facial fur, crying for the loss of life. I do not know how long I sat there and wept for the poor creature.

Howling Wolf came running to where I was sitting. He must have saw my tears and hesitated in case I was hurt more than just my arm. The other males stayed at the edge of my vision, but I only looked at Howling Wolf, using his face as my focus. He stepped closer to me and wrapped his arms around me. He rubbed my hair, letting me take comfort from him.

"It is all right, City Elf." He helped me climb out from under the bear's head. He saw my arm and called one of the other warriors over to help stop the bleeding. The warriors whispered to each other, approval in their voices.

I could not face the bear without feeling more tears well up.

"What is wrong, City Elf?" Howling Wolf asked, his voice gentle and soft.

I mimed that I killed the bear.

"I know you did. Why does that bother you so much?"

I could not figure out how to explain that the bear was innocent. I never killed something innocent before, not even when I killed in the cities.

"You killed it to protect the Clan, yes?" he asked.

I nodded, pointed to two warriors, and then mimed short.

"You saved two Clan boys by killing the bear. Would you rather have stood by and let the two boys be killed? Because we would not have made it in time if you did not get the bear away from the village."

I saw it from his point of view, as I ran my arm across my eyes to dry them.

He looked to the other warriors and said, "Let us get back to the village." He pulled away from me. "Come on, City Elf. Grandfather will need to clean and bandage that arm." I learned that the older man's title was Grandfather as he was the oldest member of the Clan. I watched as a couple of the warriors grabbed the bear, as Howling Wolf bent down and picked up my dagger and put it into its sheath. Someone else took the spear, and when everyone was ready, we walked back to the village.

Sparrow ran up to me and gave me a fierce hug. Then she yelled at me, "What in the Seven Hells were you thinking?! Taking on a bear like that?! It could have killed you!" She then noticed the bear carcass being carried by a pair of warriors. She looked to the bear, then to me, her face pale. "Did you...?"

The Elder came forward, anger all over his face. "What is the meaning of this?"

Howling Wolf answered for me. "She killed it. We got there after she slit its throat."

The Elder looked over, reassessing me.

I felt a drop of blood slide down my arm, and I tightened the bandage to try to stop the bleeding.

"She was hurt?" he asked, but I was not sure what I heard in his voice. Could it have been softness?

"Yes, Elder. The bear slashed her arm with its claws." The warrior who bandaged my arm stepped forward.

"Go take her to Grandfather," the Elder commanded Sparrow and Howling Wolf.

They walked me to the large circular building, where Grandfather was waiting for us. I saw the two boys next to the door and gave them a thumbs up or down, hoping they were all right. They both gave me a thumbs up, and I let out a sigh of relief. Howling Wolf was right in that I did the right thing by killing the bear.

"Bears are normally hibernating during this time. I wonder what caused it to wake up so early. What did the boys say?" Howling Wolf asked Grandfather.

"They say they were by the stream, and they heard a roar. They started to run, and just before they got into the village, the bear appeared out of nowhere." He unwrapped my arm, pulling the herbs the warrior put on them. Grandfather whistled at the five deep claw marks. "Do they hurt?"

I nodded, my arm throbbing in time with my heartbeat. He sat me down, and I watched him work.

"So, I heard that your eyes became blue when you heard the boys screaming. Mind telling me about it?" he asked, pulling my mind from the pain in my arm. Grandfather had been showing me how to talk with my hands, but he was the only one in the village who could read them accurately.

I told him about the deal I made with the Snow Cat, where I would give her a body to take revenge on the human who killed her kittens and herself. In return, she would help me whenever I needed her.

Sparrow and Howling Wolf tried to keep up but were not able to. "And that Snow Cat's eyes are blue?"

I nodded to him.

"Howling Wolf knew this?"

I nodded again.

"I found out the night she was trying to steal my Wolf pelt. She had blue glowing eyes, then the next morning, they were their normal green," he told Grandfather.

"Did the Snow Cat help you get away from your bondage?" Grandfather asked, but the question was not as innocent as it sounded. I thought about if I trusted these people and decided that I did. I nodded to him. "Are you willing to talk about it?"

I shook my head. I trusted them, but not that much. I especially did not want to know how they would react if they knew the full truth about me.

"Does it have to do with the larger fire fear you have?"

I nodded, willing to give him that much.

"All finished." He smiled, my arm blissfully numb and fully bandaged. "Now, that arm will be weak until it heals. So, you and Howling Wolf will need to be careful when you two spar at night."

Howling Wolf and I stiffened, not sure how Grandfather knew about those sessions.

We both looked to Sparrow. She put her hands up. "Do not look at me. I did not tell him."

"I told him." The Elder walked into the healing room. "You three thought you were being sly by waiting until nightfall to practice, but nothing goes on in this Clan without my knowledge." He pinned me with his eyes. "I allowed it because the women were saying how much of a hard worker you were, and many of them hoped you could stay." He turned to Sparrow and Howling Wolf. "Leave us." They both nodded, giving me one last look before leaving the large building. "If you want to stay in this village, you will tell Grandfather and I what you will not tell those two."

I took a deep breath, willing to get my heart rate to slow down. I asked them where to start.

"At the beginning," Grandfather said softly.

I started from my earliest memory of being sold into slavery by the City Elf Seller, and why the other City Elves called me the Cursed One. I told them about the masters I went through, how I would sacrifice my body to save other slaves, then about the master who killed the Snow Cat and her kittens. I gulped before telling them about the other deaths, the fire, and why I ran. The Elder waited in silence as Grandfather translated everything that I told them. I expected their condemnation and an immediate ejection from there if they did not choose to outright kill me.

"We need to discuss this, 13-87-22. Can you give us room by seeing what the women are making for dinner?"

I nodded, accepting the Elder's dismissal. I left the building and followed the chatter that led me to the women cooking up something delicious. I knew better than to ask what it was, because the one time I did they told me it was a snake.

One of the women, Xerinae, saw me and dragged me over to the kitchen. "Are you okay?"

I pulled up my sleeve showing them the bandages.

"Oh, Goddess Above!" one of them exclaimed.

"You did not even hesitate when you heard those screams. We all froze, yet you charged in to save those boys." Xerinae gave me a sly look. "And we heard that even the warriors were impressed. I think a few of them are going to be looking at you in a different light."

I did not like the way she sounded when saying that.

She was using her matchmaker voice and that worried me. "But we also heard that a certain warrior held you while you cried..."

Now, I really did not like what she was implying. I waved my hands in front of me, dispelling that idea.

"Dang, that would have burned Sparrow's butt if that was true." She handed me some food. "Get something to eat, since you've done more than enough today." She kicked me out of the kitchen and into the large food area.

There were people already sitting and eating, some people tried to wave me over, but I went to my normal spot next to Sparrow. "Are the gossip girls done harassing you?"

I nodded, hoping they were.

"So, what did the Elder want to talk to you about?"

I gave her a shrug that gave nothing away.

She glared at me, then at her food.

"Keep glaring, and you will sour your drink." Howling Wolf smiled at his sister before sitting across from us. He looked at my arm, but since I was using my other one to eat, he did not say anything. "Did you hear that the First Son is supposed to be returning tomorrow?" he asked Sparrow, changing the subject away from me.

She rolled her eyes. "Yes. The gossip girls have been talking about it all day." They talked about this First Son only when she was around. Any other time, they were also talking about Howling Wolf. "They say that he is ready to complete the Gauntlet, along with his friends." Her eyes tautened. "Do not go easy on them."

I looked between the two of them, confused. Who was the First Son? What was the Gauntlet?

Howling Wolf saw my confusion and explained, "The First Son is the son of the Elder, and next in line to lead the Clan. The Gauntlet is a test that all males who want to be warriors must go through to become full-fledged warriors. The First Son and this next group were in training with a couple other warriors as preparation." He gave me a grin. "Truthfully, you could beat them if you went through it."

I did not believe that, since my only training was what I got from the months I had been here. These males had been though years preparing for it. I watched as the Elder and Grandfather went in front of everyone.

"May I have your attention please." There was no hint of question in the Elder's voice. The room fell silent, waiting for his announcement. "As you all know, we had an outsider come into the village." I felt people's eyes on me, as he continued. "Today, she was willing to lay down her life for the Clan. Grandfather and I have decided that if someone is willing to die for the Clan, they should become a part of it." I felt something in my chest. Maybe it was hope? "We have also decided that she will go through the next Gauntlet to test her skills against other dangers. If she passes, she will become a Guardian for the village, standing vigilant against any persons who come to harm us."

"Father, why would you give a City Elf female the honor of being allowed in the Gauntlet?" another voice entering the dining building. Sparrow growled next to me, as she glared at the door. I looked at the newcomer, who I assumed to be the First Son. He had his father's hard face and body, but his short, tousled hair was not as dark as his father's and his eyes were too bright.

The Elder spoke, "Arrogance does not suit you, First Son. Especially when you know nothing about this decision."

I never thought the Elder would be defending me to anyone, much less his son.

"Tomorrow night, we will celebrate our newcomer. The night after, she will join you on the Gauntlet. Maybe you can see how to be a leader instead of the arrogant man you seem to have chosen to become." He and Grandfather left the dining building.

The First Son set his eyes on me, and I realized that he had a very punchable face, seeing more differences between the Elder and him. He and his friends came over to us, a smirk on his face. His voice was just above a whisper, menacing, "Just because you are sexing the Enforcer does not mean that you deserve more than what you have now. I will make sure you learn your place here, dog. When I am done with you, you will wish you never left the human cities."

Sparrow stood up, looking like she was going to attack him. Howling Wolf grabbed her. I stood up and touched her shoulder. I looked at him in the eyes, before giving him my familiar rude gesture, telling him that he and friends did not scare me.

He looked like he was going to hit me but stopped himself from going through with it. He got in really close to me and said, "You will see just how wrong you are for being here." He looked to his friends. "Time to go."

Elves whispered around us, the entire dining building watching us. I glared at the food left on my plate before I took off on my own. I needed to calm down so the Snow Cat could rest in her den, since I knew I would need her in two days. I walked to the river, letting myself rage near the shoreline. He reminded me too much of the masters I served and subsequently killed. I was passed from master to master after a series of deaths against those who owned me. There was no way to pin their deaths on me, so I was just passed through the royal courts.

A shuffle sounded behind me, and I grabbed the dagger's hilt with my non-dominant hand. I whipped around, pulling it out at arm's length, and threw it.

Howling Wolf caught it between his hands. He walked back over to me, handing it back. "Are you all right?"

I shook my head, miming wanting to punch someone in the face.

"He has that effect on Sparrow as well." He sat on the bank of the river and patted the ground next to him.

I sat down and stared out at the dark water.

"It is funny, because the three of us used to be close friends."

I made a disgusted face, and he just laughed.

"He was a good man growing up, until his mother was killed by another Clan. He hardened his heart after that and became the asshole you saw today. The old him would have never said anything like that."

He looked at me, as I calmed down and said, "You know that you can talk to Sparrow and me about anything, right? We are not going to judge you for your past. We know that you have been through things that none of us could imagine having to go through. Yet you survived, and by fate, you attacked me instead of another Wood Elf." He lightly punched me in the non-injured arm. "Even though you almost won, I am glad that I was able to beat you."

I laughed silently at that since he completely kicked my ass.

He sobered up. "I cannot help you with the Gauntlet, more than what I have already taught you. I also cannot tell you what the challenge of the Gauntlet is, but I can tell you that you have survived tougher situations." I yawned, my energy and anger spent. "Sparrow said to come get you to bed, so that you can rest up for tomorrow. Grandfather says that your arm will be better by the start of the Gauntlet, so no worries there." He stood up, and then helped me stand up.

He walked us back to the village, dropping me off with Sparrow. She pulled me inside, where the gossip girls were sitting everywhere. "They think there is something going on between you and my brother. Can you explain what you have been doing, so they will stop annoying me?"

I nodded to her, then mimed that Howling Wolf had been teaching me to fight.

"And tonight? After you left dinner?"

I mimed that we talked.

"Anything more salacious than that?" Xerinae hoped.

I shook my head.

"So, you two are not laying together like the First Son said?"

I shook my head again; she seemed crestfallen.

"See? Nothing has been going on. The First Son has no idea what he is talking about. Now, can you girls leave, so I can check her wound before bed?" Sparrow ushered them out of her house.

Xerinae looked at my shirt. "Pass it, so I can repair it."

I took it off and handed it to her.

"As for what the First Son said about you wishing you never left the humans, he was an ass for saying it. We are glad to have you here, City Elf." She bounced on her feet, excitement radiating from her. "Maybe she will get a name tomorrow night! I mean the warriors get them when they bring back their first kill. Since she killed the bear, I bet that counts!"

"Only if the Elder and Grandfather agreed to that. You just try telling them to give her one," Sparrow replied. "She is also going to need clothes for tomorrow night. Think you have anything that would fit her?"

Xerinae grinned. "I am sure I can find something." She stood up and stretched, with the rest of the gossip girls. Just before she left, she tossed a comment over her shoulder. "Maybe I can find something that will help Howling Wolf see her as a potential wife." She shut the door quickly, as Sparrow's shoe hit it.

Sparrow retrieved her shoe and looked at me. "They mean well, but Goddess Above. She has been trying to set my brother up for decades now. She does not understand that he will not go for just any woman because his heart is already taken."

I tilted my head to ask her to explain more.

She huffed. "Get changed, and we will discuss it."

I changed into the bed clothes and climbed into my side of the fluffy bed.

She climbed into her side. "So, you really want to know?"

I nodded.

"There was a woman named Resting Doe. Doe was easily the most beautiful woman in the Clan. He was courting her, hoping to be her husband. She was in training to become the next Healer, but one day, she just up and disappeared."

I looked at her, concerned.

"She ran away from the Clan in order to be a male from another Clan." I mimed a gasp. "She was in the forest, where she fell in love with another warrior. They met in secret for a while before she decided to join his Clan." She gripped the blankets hard. "It is because of her that I warn women off. It is not just for him; it is also for the women who could never get his heart. I do not want someone waiting for him if he cannot fix the heart that Doe broke."

I pat her on the arm, trying to give comfort to her anger.

She smiled at me. "Please do not take this the wrong way, but at first, I did not want you near my brother because I thought you were temporary. But I wonder if by warning women off, that I was not allowing him to heal. Since you are permanent, maybe he can learn to love, just by you keeping his heart warm. Even if he does not love you or you him, he laughs more when you are around. He is more of himself when you are around, and I want that for him."

I gave her a light punch in the arm.

"Fine! I will let women see him as available."

I smiled, letting her know she was doing the right thing for him.

She grinned as she pushed me into the pillows with her. "Get to sleep. Tomorrow is going to be a long night, then an early morning."

Chapter 05

We woke up when Xerinae knocked on Sparrow's door.

Sparrow opened it, and the other woman flounced in. "I fixed your shirt!" She tossed it at me as I sat up and then turned to Sparrow. "Elder has given everyone the day off in preparation for tonight. But you and I are to get our City Elf ready for it." She looked at me, and I was not sure I liked the predatory look in her eyes. "Grandfather said that she is to wear what women would during our namings."

"But we are named when we begin bleeding yearly," Sparrow pointed out.

"Correct, but the clothing is the same."

I looked between the two women, trying to decipher what they were saying.

"I found something that will make the males want to see what is hidden under it."

"You are still not trying to make my brother see her naked, are you?" Sparrow mumbled.

I was not sure whether to tell her that he already had.

Xerinae caught my look and said, "She has got a secret." She grinned. "Has Howling Wolf seen you naked?"

I nodded, and Sparrow glared at me like I cursed her ancestors. I quickly mimed about the river and needing to get warm, or we would die.

Sparrow looked relieved while Xerinae was aggravated. "That is not what we meant at all!" she grumbled.

I mimed that he did not see me as a woman, but as a friend, and maybe a fellow fighter. Sparrow laughed, as Xerinae kept grumbling about Howling Wolf was hopeless.

Someone knocked on the door, and they jumped into covering me up with the blanket. "Hey, Sparrow, can I talk to you?" Howling Wolf asked through the door.

"Yeah, give me a second." She gave a threatening gesture to Xerinae and I. She walked out the door, leaving the two of us in her house. We both ran to the door to listen in, as I changed into regular clothes. "What is going on, Wolf?"

"Since the Gauntlet starts tomorrow, she is required to stay in the barracks house with the rest of the candidates."

"And you are worried about her there, right?" Sparrow asked him.

"Extremely worried. We have never had a female go through the Gauntlet, so this is new territory for us. I am especially worried because the First Son and his friends will also be in the barracks house. I do not trust them to not do anything to her."

I opened the door and closed it behind me.

Howling Wolf glanced my way. "Is your arm feeling better?"

I nodded.

"You were eavesdropping?" Sparrow accused.

I shrugged. The warrior that wrapped my arm up stood near the edge of the house. I waved at him, and he waved back.

He came over. "I am just here because we do not want the accusation of favoritism, since he is not allowed to talk about the Gauntlet tasks themselves."

"Will there be any males that would be able to make sure she is not hurt?" Sparrow asked him.

"The only people there will be her, along with the First Son and his friends, since they are the only Candidates this round."

Howling Wolf looked like he wanted to stop this from happening.

"Have you talked with Grandfather about this?" she asked.

"He and the Elder are the ones who decided about the barracks." He grimaced.

I looked at him, touching his cheek with my palm, as I got an idea. I mimed about seeing the barracks for myself now.

"You are supposed to be getting ready for tonight."

I waved that off since this was more important.

"I cannot show you."

"But I can." The other warrior smirked. "You cannot because you cannot show favoritism, but I can because I am not a part of the Gauntlet." He grabbed my arm, leading me toward the barracks, "I am Raven, by the way. Nice to meet you officially, City Elf."

I smiled back.

He led me to a long building and opened the door. It was completely empty, save for the line of beds, the water closet in the back, and the chest at the foot of each bed. "I cannot help with finding a place for you, though," he admitted.

So, the sleeping part is a part of the Gauntlet itself. I needed to keep that in mind. I looked around, trying to figure out the answer to this conundrum. I saw the rafters above and got an idea. Snow Cats like heights, so I had been practicing my jumping into trees and high places. I could reach the rafters to sleep. But I did not tell Raven. He might be on my side for this, but I did not want to take the chance of anyone figuring out what I was thinking. I nodded to him, and he walked me back to Sparrow's house.

"She thinks that she found something."

I nodded in agreement.

There was visible relief in Howling Wolf's eyes. "Then, I will let you get back to getting ready, while we go tell the other Candidates that they will be staying in the barracks tonight as well. Stay safe."

We went back inside the house, and Xerinae scrunched her face in concern. "If she is staying in the barracks with the other Candidates, maybe we should not whet the male appetite. I do not trust them not to hurt her if they saw her as something except another warrior."

The wheels turned in Sparrow's mind, as a smile blossomed on her face. "Get the girls. We are going a different route. They need to see her as a warrior, so we are going to make her into one."

We came out of Sparrow's house as the drums played, calling us to the ceremony. They clothed me in all red linen, leathers hidden underneath for warmth. I wore the Bear pelt at my back, its head lying on top of mine. The red tunic and leggings were accented with copper threads and beads. They dressed my long hair up with dark red ribbons wrapping through the braid. They painted my face with makeup, highlighting my facial features, bringing out the colors of my eyes and painting my lips dark red. We walked through the village, the women in front of me, to present me to the Elder as the ceremonial guest of honor. The drums echoed through the forest, pulling us toward them.

I saw the men dancing around the fire, welcoming a new Clan member. Xerinae said they did this every time someone was named. The drums stopped as we reached the edge of the circle. The women stayed around me, playing the part of the Goddess. The men, playing as the Dark Consort, went and gathered the women, one by one, taking them by the hand, until I was the only one left. I took a step forward, challenging the men in their taking of the women. They challenged back, hiding the women in the center of their circle.

The women explained the steps to me as they were getting me ready. I was not actually supposed to fight them, just the challenge was enough to get them to see the power I held. One by one, the men released the captured women, as they gathered behind me, accepting my protection of them. The men parted as I moved toward the Elder and Grandfather.

I saw Howling Wolf in all black standing next to them, and surprise flashed across his eyes. He was the final challenger, the one who taught me everything I need to know for the naming and Gauntlet. I raised my hand up to him, calling him to the challenge. He took his three steps forward, entering the circle of movement with me. We circled each other. He reached forward to grab me, playing the part of danger that would always be there. I let him grab me, then snagged his wrist and pulled him away from me. His question was if I was ready to defend the Clan with everything I was. I answered his movements with the promise to protect them until the day I died. He moved to the side, allowing me to pass.

I looked to the Elder and Grandfather and saw them pleased that I followed their traditions. I knelt in front of them, acknowledging their position and respect for it. "Here kneels a woman ready to claim her name," the Elder called out to the crowd. "She has fought off a Bear to protect her fellow Clansmen." He looked to Howling Wolf and Sparrow. "As her closest people, do you have a name for her?"

I did not know they would be the ones to name me, and I wondered why they did not tell me.

"We do, Honorable Elder." Sparrow stepped forward. "Our Clanswoman carries the spirit of a Snow Cat within her. In light of this, we have chosen her name."

"Speak her name," the Elder commanded.

Howling Wolf's voice was strong and clear. "We give her the name of Silent Snow, in honor of the deadly silence they share when they hunt, telling no prey of their presence."

"Silent Snow, do you accept your name, the one given to you by those closest to you?" Grandfather asked.

I gave him a single nod, taking the name they thought suited me best.

He helped me to stand. "We accept Silent Snow as our newest member of our Clan. Tonight, we feast and rejoice on this honorable occasion!" Grandfather called out to the rest of the Clan.

The Clan cheered, happy that I had been named. They could finally stop calling me City Elf or the designation branded on my wrist.

The Clan dismissed to enjoy the rest of the party, I turned to the Elder. I took off the Bear pelt and presented it to him.

He tilted his head. "What is this?"

I spoke with my hands, as Grandfather translated. "A gift for the male who gave her the greatest gift she could have ever received."

I smiled. The Elder took the Bear pelt from me, and I could see a hint of tears in his eyes.

"It is funny that you are giving him this." Grandfather stepped closer to touch both the Elder's and my shoulders. "You see, he was named Ferocious Bear by his wife, after he became a man," he told me quietly.

I watched as the Elder wiped his tears away before they could fall.

The Elder pulled off the Snow Cat pelt from his back and gave it to me. "This should fit you better, Silent Snow." He settled the Bear pelt on his shoulders, then spoke, "Go enjoy your night, Silent Snow. Tomorrow is the start of a new task for you."

I nodded, taking his dismissal. I hopped over to Sparrow and Howling Wolf as they laughed with Raven and Xerinae. They saw the Snow Cat pelt, then turned to see the Elder with the Bear one.

"He looks so happy," Sparrow commented. She turned and gave me a hug. "I am so glad that you are officially a part of the Clan, Silent Snow." She grinned. "Now, we dance!" She dragged me out to the dance circle and showed me the steps.

I followed along while I got the hang of it. The music sped up; our feet and arms were flying. Then the music stopped, and I fell to the ground.

Howling Wolf came over and gave me a hand to stand back up. "Sparrow should have warned you that dance has a sudden stop."

I smiled, feeling exhilarated from the ceremony and dances.

"You look a bit flushed, Snow." He led me to a table, where Sparrow, Xerinae, and Raven sat. He handed me a mug of water, "Drink up."

I sipped on the water, watching the other dancers.

Food was served, and I found out what Bear tasted like. It was not bad, but I prayed over the meal, another apology to the Bear, hoping it would find its way to rebirth. I listened to them talk about their own naming ceremonies and the shenanigans that happened during them. I felt at home, and for once in my life, at peace and safe. They gave me more than just a name, they gave me a family. I watched as people yawned and retired, but I was told that I had to wait with the other Candidates for instructions for the morning.

I waved goodbye to Sparrow and Xerinae as they went back to their homes.

A voice snarled behind me, "A name? Like a City Elf deserves a name." I turned to glare at the First Son, as he continued, "I heard that City Elf females are only good for breeding and being on their backs."

A memory of a City Elf girl being raped flashed through my mind. I stood up, fully ready to attack him like he deserved.

"Enough, First Son," Howling Wolf commanded. "Stand down, Silent Snow."

I crossed my arms over my chest but did as he said. One of the other warriors was passing around drinks to the Candidates. I grabbed the mug from the platter, watching as the other Candidates grabbed theirs. We waited for the next instruction.

Howling Wolf stood us all get closer together but kept the First Son and I as far away as possible from each other. Behind us, circled the other warriors. "Drink this cup only if you believe you are ready for the Gauntlet. Once you have sipped from it, you are no longer allowed to back out." He waited for any of us to step aside. We all just waited, looking at him. He held his own mug up. "We drink to the newest Candidates and to the perils of the Gauntlet!" he shouted, the warriors around us answering the shout.

I took a sip from the cup before I recognized the taste. I threw the mug on the ground, as I watched the other Candidates fall, only to be caught by one of the standing warriors. I tried to fight off the sleeping poison, but even that small sip was too much. I glared at Howling Wolf, seeing the sympathy in his eyes. I wanted to hit him, but all I could muster was mouthing, "You Bastard," to him.

"I'm sorry, Snow," he said as darkness enclosed around me. I was gone before I ever hit the ground.

Chapter 06

I woke up, fighting against the sleep poison. I bit my tongue, the pain keeping me awake. We were in a covered caravan, reminding me all too much of the travelling slave cages. It was daylight out, and I noticed the other Candidates still out. My wrists and ankles were tied in front of me, and I glared at Howling Wolf and another warrior sitting with him. He did not say anything to me, but I could see the pain in his eyes.

The other warrior remarked to the Enforcer, "I am surprised she shook that off so quickly. I do not think any of the other Candidates have been able to do that."

I spoke with my hands, telling them that I knew what it was by taste, so I did not get the full dosage.

They both stiffened, not realizing anyone would have tasted it. Howling Wolf asked gently. "The humans used it on you?"

I gave him an angry nod, feeling the rage from the last time I drank a sleeping poison and the damage it caused me. There was regret on his face, like he would not have done it if he knew. I could feel the Snow Cat stumbling up, the spirit shaking off the poison as well.

My eyes tinted blue, but Howling Wolf spoke softly, "Not yet."

I pulled my lips back in a hiss.

"Since she is the first to awaken, she is the first to be dropped off." The other warrior knocked on the wood between our compartment and the driver. I shook my head, forcing them to look at me. If they tried to toss me out, I would fight back with everything I was. "You do not want to be the first one out? But that puts you closer to the village." I gave him a look of death before he looked away. "Or maybe we should knock her back out until the others awaken?"

Howling Wolf mumbled just loud enough for me to hear, "Do not run away, Snow."

I gave him a sadistic smile. No, I would not run away, but he would need the entire continent between us to protect him. I looked to see the First Son near my foot, and I thought about kicking him in the face. The wagon kept moving, until the other Candidates stirred. Then the wagon stopped, and they carried us out and laid us on the ground in the middle of the forest. Howling Wolf was gentle with me, maybe hoping that I would forgive him. Maybe I would, but that would not be today.

When the others awakened, Howling Wolf said, "Your task is to find your way back to the village. You will be alone out here with your fellow Candidates, so I suggest learning how to work together. If you try to go this alone, it will be much tougher than you think it will be." He shifted his gaze to the First Son and I. "Along the way, there will be dangers that you have to overcome, so I suggest that you plan for them."

He then laid different weapons on the ground near us, "Each of you will get a weapon that you have been deemed an expert of." The other warriors left, leaving only the Enforcer with us. "Take this task seriously. We will not be here to save you if you get into trouble. You will have to rely on your fellow Candidates. Good luck to all of you." He walked back through the forest, leaving us all tied up.

I glanced at the pile of weapons, seeing a spear that would work for me. I felt the dagger in its sheath and wondered why they would not take it. Unless they did not realize that I carried it with me everywhere. I lifted the bottom of my dark red linen shirt and grabbed the dagger, cutting the cords around my wrists and ankles. I stood up and grabbed the spear.

"You are just going to leave us?!" The First Son growled as I walked away. "And why do you have a dagger, but we do not?"

I shrugged, not able to give him an answer.

"You can at least help us, before you take off back to the humans where you belong."

Again, I looked at the weapons and found a knife that I could leave. I used the knife to undo their ankles but left their wrists. They should be able to get out of those without my help. I did not want them near me with weapons while we were all alone. I tossed the knife to the ground, before walking into the forest. The breeze caressed me, and I smiled, feeling better than before. The sounds of the other Candidates getting out of their binds drifted to me, so I took off through the forest, letting the Snow Cat guide my steps. The Gauntlet had started.

Chapter 07

It was day three of the Gauntlet, and the other Candidates were no closer than I was to getting back to the village. I slept in the trees away from them, so that they could not attack me at night. I know Howling Wolf said to trust them, but I could not.

I reached the river before they did, and I saw them a little bit further upriver. We needed to cross it, but the other Candidates spoke with confidence that they could swim across it. The First Son went first since he was their designated leader. He slipped in the river from the tall bank. Something felt wrong as he fell below the waterline. I looked at the rushing water and knew what happened. The undercurrent was too strong for him to swim through.

The Snow Cat took over, assessing our surroundings. I looked around to find somewhere downstream, as his friends tried to grab him from the water. I saw a tree hanging over the river and ran to it, hoping to make it in time. I did not like the male, but if he was going to die, I wanted it to be the one to kill him. I bounced on the tree, testing its strength and limberness. I wrapped my legs around the tree, linking my ankles together.

I swung under it, wrapping my arms around the spear to hold it easier and to keep it from falling from my wet hands.

The First Son rushed toward me, trying to stay above the waterline. I whistled at him, getting his and his friends' attention.

He grabbed for the spear just as he passed under the tree I was hanging from. "Do not let go of me," he begged as he wrapped his arms around the spear, and I grabbed onto his wrists.

I held onto him, while his friends came to the tree I was on and tried to figure out how to get to us. I did not think that far ahead, only caring about the width being able for me to keep my ankles tight against one another. Someone tossed a vine over me and the tree, dangling in the water below. He reached for it, then wrapped it around his arm. He and I kept a death grip on each other with his other arm.

"Let go! We got him!" his friends shouted.

I nodded to him below me.

He shook his head, fear in his eyes, "No!"

I readjusted my grip to hold the spear with the inside of my elbow, as I used that arm to try to pull myself up. The First Son kept a hold of the spear and the vine. I would not be able to keep holding him there, nor would he have the strength to hold on for much longer.

I took a deep breath and let go of the tree with my ankles. I splashed into the water next to him, grabbing onto the vine as I dropped. His friends pulled us to the safety of the shoreline. They pulled the two of us onto the bank, and the First Son looked like he had stared the Dark Consort in the eyes, just for Him to let the Elf go. I laid on the bank, breathing hard, staring at the trees above. My vision went back to normal, the Snow Cat going back into her den. If they attacked me, I would not be able to fight back at that second.

The First Son sat up before I did and just looked at me. "Why did you save me?" he asked quietly.

I looked up at him from where I laid on the ground. I shrugged, not being able to give him a good answer.

"Even after all I said to you, and all of the insults I flung at you, you still saved me." He leaned over me, "Thank you, Silent Snow."

I gave him a thumbs up, before I felt good enough to sit up myself.

I looked at the river, trying to figure out how to cross it. I looked at the tree and thought about how strong it had been. It could hold the weight of two of us, and it spanned the width of the river. I grabbed my spear from next to me and walked to the tree. I got on it and bounced on it a couple more times. The wood bent, but just as strong as before. I whistled to the other Candidates and walked across, carefully keeping my steps from leaning me one way of another. I reached the other side and waved to them. I waited until they all were across and then took off on my own again.

Night fell and I sat in the tree above the other Candidates, not letting them out of my sight.

The First Son came over to where I was sitting, holding a bowl up to me. "You do not have to stay away from us. We are not going to hurt you."

I looked down at the First Son, debating if I believed him. I hopped out of the tree, deciding that since he owed me his life, he would not try to take mine. I landed next to him, taking the bowl from him as a gesture of good faith. We walked back to the fire, and everyone was silent from what had happened earlier.

I took off the leathers from under the red linens and let them dry above the fire with the First Son's clothes. After a while, they talked amongst themselves about the training they had received to prepare for this. I listened as they talked about the jokes and games had they played on each other. They brought up memories, laughing as they told stories about each other.

Soon, they yawned, and one by one they fell asleep. Only the First Son, and I were still awake.

"I am sorry for everything I said and put you through. You did not deserve it. I guess I was just worried that if a City Elf female could finish the Gauntlet, then it would not be worth as much as I thought it was." He looked me in the eyes, and I saw the guilt in them.

I lightly punched him in the shoulder as I smiled.

He returned a sad one. "We should keep watch."

I motioned that I would take the first watch and would wake him for the second one.

He yawned and stretched out.

I watched the fire, listening for sounds that did not belong in the forest. All was quiet and soon, I yawned myself. I stood up and stretched, which helped] me stay awake. When it was time to switch, I tapped the First Son on the shoulder, and he took over. I debated if I should go into the trees, but he explained that he would not let anything harm me or his friends. With that promise, I curled up and fell asleep next to the fire.

It was day five of the Gauntlet, and we were now working together as a team. The group had designated me as scout and second-in-command, since I had proven myself to them. I went into the trees to see if I could find the next dangers that lay in wait for us. We came across a clearing of tall grass, where we saw a camp set up. I did not like the feeling the camp site gave me. I told them to wait in the forest while I investigated. They had learned what each of my whistles meant, so they would come if I needed help or deemed it safe.

I walked to the campsite, scanning the area. There were five tents set up, but there were only three packs. The other Candidates were good at hunting and fishing, so I did not worry about having to eat. The lack of two packs bothered me a little. Where were they? I searched around, trying to see if I could find them, when whooping and hollering emerged from the forest.

I dove into the grass, as three men bring out two of the Candidates, except the First Son and three others. I watched as the three invaders brought them into the tall grass clearing. I whistled a bird song, letting the other Candidates know I was there. The three invaders looked around for the source of the sound.

I laid in the tall grass until nightfall, letting the Snow Cat take over my vision with her blue tinged night vision. I went back into the forest, finding the other four Candidates in the trees.

"They snuck up on them as we were trying to get into the trees. What do we do?" the First Son asked.

Besides an all-out assault? I had no idea. The clearing was not large, so we could surround it easily enough. I mimed them shooting arrows, and they agreed that they would be able to. I told them my plan, and they agreed that it could go wrong in so many ways, but it was the best I had. They went to their designated spots.

The First Son stayed near me. "Are you sure about this?" he asked, worried about his friends.

I shrugged but nodded as well.

"Just give us the sign when you are ready." He climbed into the tree next to me.

I waited until I got signals that everyone was ready. I grabbed my spear and walked into the clearing.

"What is this?" One of the invaders asked his friends.

"Looks like a City Elf," another mumbled.

The third stood up to face me. "But look at that hair! City Elves don't have silver hair!"

I pulled my hair behind my ears, showing them the delicate points of them.

"She is a City Elf!" I came into the area of their fire, my eyes blue. "She has got pretty eyes, too!" I looked to the two captured Candidates. The invaders caught my looks. "You came to see what we have?"

I nodded once, closing my eyes, letting my hearing take over.

The invaders came up closer to me, looking at the clothes I wore and just my overall look. "I bet she could fetch us a lot of money in the cities if we sold her."

I opened my eyes, and in one smooth motion, grabbed my dagger and threw it into the ground. I whistled sharply and arrows came from around them, striking into the dirt near the invaders. I whistled again, and they stopped.

The three invaders looked at me. "What in the Seven Hells?"

I kept my eyes on them but was able to see the other two Candidates in the background, cutting their bindings with the knife I threw to the ground. Once they were free, I whistled again. Arrows plunged into the shoulders of the invaders, dropping them to the ground. I grabbed my dagger and the other two Candidates to run. I knew the other four were keeping an eye so that we could escape without issue.

We met with the rest of the group near the river. They all talked about what just happened. "So, you were bait?" one of the captured Candidates asked.

I smiled and nodded.

"You are insane, Snow; they could have killed you," the other replied.

"It was the only plan we had. She knew that they would want to try to capture her to sell, so we used that," the First Son explained. "Trust us, we did not like the plan either, but it worked." We followed the river downstream, trying to see if we could see the village in the distance. We were still too far away, so we set up camp for the night.

Chapter 08

It has been a week since the Gauntlet began, and I was starting to wear down. The other Candidates were just as weary from the constant walking.

How far away were we from the village? I kept asking myself.

We ended up stopping early, hoping the break would revive our spirits and strength. We fell asleep, not realizing that another danger was just on the horizon.

We woke up to a splash of water to the face. I jumped up, the blue tint covering my vision. We were surrounded. I glared at the Candidate who was supposed to keep watch, seeing the water drip from his face and nose.

The people laughed at me as I glared at them. There must have been twenty of them against the seven of us. "Well, look at this. The City Elf thinks she is tough."

I spat on the ground at him. The other Candidates looked between the leader and I.

"See, boss? I knew that we would have a good hunting trip this time." A lacky smiled.

I reached for my dagger, still hidden under my clothes.

"Oh, she wants to fight?" The leader and his posse laughed. "Then come at me, City Elf. Let us see what you got." He grabbed a knife from one of his people, while I grabbed my dagger from its sheath.

I motioned for the other Candidates to stand up. They did as I asked, waiting for my signal.

"Oh, she is the boss bitch." The leader grinned. "It will be fun to break you."

We circled each other, before he was in front of the other Candidates, and I was in front of his posse. I whistled and the other Candidates grabbed the leader, holding his own knife to his throat. The lackeys grabbed me, but I fought back, tossing the dagger in the air, and caught it hilt up. I slammed the blade behind me, slashing at anyone who got near me. I watched as the other Candidates subdued the leader, but I was overpowered.

Someone slashed my arm. "Let him go, and we might let your bitch live." The lacky who gave the leader his knife held one to my throat.

I shook my head and mouthed for them to run and get help. I would rather they leave me behind than get trapped with me.

The other Candidates looked at me, and their emotions warred on their faces. It would have been easier if they still hated me, because then they would not have hesitated to leave me behind. They followed my lead, tying up the leader, before grabbing their weapons to leave.

The lackey pushed me forward onto the ground, my silver hair glinting in the sunlight. "It is her! It is the Kinkiller!"

I saw my dagger on the ground and grabbed it. I made a come at me motion to them. Without the other Candidates being in the crossfire, I let the Snow Cat take over. I dodged around different attacks, before slashing and stabbing. It took some time, but only the slaver leader was left.

Bodies and blood littered the area around me. Some had arrows sticking from their chests and bodies. I wondered why when a twig snapped behind me, and I threw my dagger.

Howling Wolf deflected it into the ground.

I saw the other Candidates' wide eyes and the look of fear in their faces. The warriors with them looked at the slaughter around me, understanding what I was. Howling Wolf stepped toward me, as the Snow Cat went into her den. I glared at the people dead on the ground around me and felt no remorse for them.

"What is this, Snow?"

I gave him a blank stare; he looked away first.

"What is going on, Howling Wolf?" the First Son asked.

"We had reports of slavers in the area, so we decided to check on it. I see that you found some." His voice held a bit of approval, until he looked at me. "Your life is not worthless, so you need to stop trying to throw it away, even if it is to save others."

"With all due respect, Howling Wolf, her life was never truly at stake." First Son stood up for me. "She may be reckless, but she always knew that she could count on us to protect her, just as she has done for us."

"Would you be saying that if you knew that the lackey was going to slit her throat?" Howling Wolf asked harshly. "Or what if the blade she was cut with was poisoned?" He looked at my bleeding arm. "You act like she is a leader, when you should be the one who bosses them around."

"We share leadership," the First Son snapped back. "We know how to survive in the forest by hunting and fishing. She knows how to fight better than we can when it comes to close range maneuvers. Therefore, we defer to her when it comes to her matter of expertise. A true leader does not boss people

79

around. They are willing to step up and protect their people at all costs."

Howling Wolf looked to the two of us. "I guess something good came from this." He turned back to the other warriors and asked, "Is the First Son right in what he says leadership is?"

The humor in his voice was evident now. The warriors raised their voices in approval.

"I am glad that you have finally grown in your role as a leader, First Son. Your father would be proud, as would your mother. She had a strength that your father lacked. She believed in protecting her people at all costs, even laying her life down for those ideals." He set his hand on his friend's shoulder, "You all have passed the Gauntlet. " Howling Wolf turned at me. "Do you want me to take a look at it?"

I pulled my lips back into a hiss, before walking away from all of them. Then I grabbed my dagger from the ground and wiped my own blood off it, stomping into the forest. I needed to get away from them, away from the anger that stayed with me. Slavers were in the area... That would explain the people we kept running into, but why were they this far away from the cities? I went to the river and cleaned the dagger in it.

"Snow?" Howling Wolf asked. He came up next to me, and I turned away from him, still pissed that he used a sleep poison on me. "I am sorry, Snow. I did not know that you had it used on you before. I did not know what was done to you while under its influence."

I shot a glare at him, but he put his hands up in front of him defensively.

"Grandfather told me in confidence after I saw your reaction to it. He told me about what you told him and the Elder."

I stood up and stalked away from him, my feelings too raw to deal with people at that moment. The memories washed over me, the sleep poison, the rapes, the tortures, all of it. I killed my previous masters because of what they did to me and other slaves. Humans have short memories and lives, so I was able to kill them without being found out. But those deaths did not erase the pain that came from those wounds. Then when someone I trusted used it on me... It reopened those old wounds. I shuddered, and a sob escaped from me. I tried to stop myself, but the tears would not stop. I ran away from the humans, but I was forever tainted by them.

Howling Wolf and the other warriors and Candidates gave me my space, as they interrogated the leader of the slavers who were in the area. I was empty and numb as I walked back to them. The slaver looked at me, before I saw his eyes widen.

"I knew I recognized you! You are 13-87-22! There is a bounty on your head to return you to your masters." He looked to the other Wood Elves. "If you return her, my employer can make it worth your while."

I took my dagger and slashed him across the throat, giving my anger and rage give force to the cut. He gagged on his own blood, as I walked away, toward where I knew the village was. No one stopped me or came near me. My eyes were clear, so they knew that it was not the Snow Cat spirit that killed the slaver. I wanted to hunt down every slaver in the forest and kill them, but I did not know if Howling Wolf would let me, much less allow me out of his sight.

They followed me toward the village, but night came before we reached it. I climbed into a tree away from everyone, letting myself stew in my misery. I leaned back against the trunk, while the warriors' voices drifted from below me. The Candidates were telling them about everything that had happened.

I ignored them, instead, pulling inwards to see three thousand years of memories. I was barely a third of the way through my long life, and I already wanted to die. Maybe that is why I kept putting my life on the line? If something killed me, then at least I would not have to deal with the pain of the past any longer.

The tree shook as Howling Wolf climbed up to the branch behind me, "We need to talk." I did not answer him, so he continued. "I told you that you could trust Sparrow and I with everything and that we would not judge you for your past. Today, that past and the present collided. We watched as you killed that slaver in cold blood. I did not think you could have that kind of blankness in you, but what we saw scared us." He looked around the trunk of the tree "Silent Snow, are we able to trust you?"

I was not expecting that kind of question, so I did not answer. I wanted to nod and let him know that they were all safe from me, but was that not what I was running from all day? The memories of those I killed? Did I worry that I would lose control and kill those closest to me? Is that why I needed to be alone? I turned around the trunk of the tree, so he could see my movements. I shrugged.

He climbed over to the branch I was sitting on and asked, "What did the slaver mean about you having a bounty on you?"

I spoke with my hands, moving slowly so he could keep up. I told him that I had killed many of my human masters before I ran away. I did not give him an exact number, but he understood that it was a high body count. I grabbed my braided hair and held it to the moonlight, reminding him that it was not normal for a City Elf to have silver hair. As far as I knew, I was the only one.

"Are you going to run away again, or come back to the village with us?" He grabbed my hands in his. "Please say that you will come back to the village."

I had nowhere else to go, so I told him I would go back to the village. Something changed between us, as he saw how cold I could be and how easily I would kill. Question was on how much it bothered him, knowing that much about me.

We reached the village the next mid-day. The entire rest of the walk, everyone stayed away from me, except the First Son and Howling Wolf. They both tried to talk to me, but after rebuffing them several times, they too left me alone. I was not riding the hatred as I was yesterday, but I still pushed them away from me. We came back as new warriors, so a celebration was to happen that night.

Sparrow and Xerinae tried to rope me into wearing whatever they were originally planning, but Howling Wolf stopped them.

I went to see Grandfather, because even though he told Howling Wolf about me, I trusted him the most. "You should be celebrating with the other Candidates." He then saw my face and sat me down in a chair. "What seems to be the issue, Silent Snow?" he asked as he gave me a cup of warm tea.

I set the cup down and told him what happened with the slavers in the forest. He just waited until I finished before saying anything.

"You are worried that they do not see you as a warrior, but instead as a murderer? And I think you also are worried about how Howling Wolf sees you now?"

I nodded and sipped on the tea he gave me, letting its flavor stay on my tongue.

"Have they explained to you how Howling Wolf became the Enforcer?"

I shook my head.

"Maybe you should ask him about it. You might discover that you two have more in common than you know." He helped me stand up. "Go talk to him." He wrinkled his nose. "But first, I suggest going into the spring and scrubbing your adventures off your skin." He smiled, as he teased me.

I gave him a small one back, before heading toward the still water spring like he suggested. I took off the leathers and red linens I wore. I kept the dagger within easy reach, as I stepped into the cold water. I shivered but dove in anyway. Once my body acclimated, I took the fine sand from the bottom of the spring to scrub my skin. I scrubbed the blood off first, before checking the cut on my arm. I used that sand to scrub in my hair, cleaning it of the Gauntlet. I dove back under the water and washed off the blood and sand.

I stood up in time to see the First Son standing on the bank. He was staring at the scars that covered my body. I ignored him, grabbed the linens, and cleaned them in the spring.

He walked over to me. "Some of these are old..."

I just nodded, as he touched one on my upper back.

"How long were you with the humans?"

I thought about what the Elder and Grandfather figured from when I lost my voice. I held up a two then a seven.

"Twenty-seven hundred years? How old are you?"

I gave him a three and a zero.

"So, you were three hundred when you were first taken?"

I nodded.

"No wonder you killed the slavers with that dead look in your eyes." He almost sounded impressed.

I finished cleaning the linens and twisted the fabric to get as much water out of them as possible. I put the cold clothes back on.

"Does Howling Wolf know about them?"

I nodded since he had seen me nude before.

"No wonder he thought that you could handle the Gauntlet. I am guessing that after all you have lived through, it was easy."

I shook my head, grinning at him. I mimed saving him and the other Candidates as the hard work it was. Then I mimed that they could hunt and fish, and I could not.

He just laughed. "You were hopeless without us. Could not even catch a bunny on your own."

Sparrow walked over to us and said, "Grandfather says that you would be out here." She stopped when she saw the First Son laughing so hard, he was crying. "What did you do to him?"

I shrugged, as he sobered back up. "We were discussing how she is the worst hunter I have ever seen."

Sparrow stayed wary of him. He saw her take the mental step back from him. "Sparrow, I wanted to apologize for the way I treated you. You were one of my best friends, and I took that friendship and smashed it to pieces. I can never hope to have your forgiveness, but I wanted you to know that I regret everything I did to hurt you."

She looked to him, then to me. "Snow, can you give us space? Grandfather says that you need to find and talk to Howling Wolf."

I nodded to her, grabbed my stuff, dressed, and went back to the village.

The celebration was dying down, and the cold wind blew through the wet linens. I sat near the fire, letting its warmth help me dry. Howling Wolf laid his heavy wolf pelt across my shoulders and back.

"Grandfather said you wanted to talk to me?" His voice was neutral as he sat next to me.

I nodded but did not know how to ask it.

"You want to know how I became the Enforcer?" Grandfather must have told him my question when he sent him to me.

He leaned forward, putting his elbows on his thighs. "An Enforcer is designated when a warrior kills a lot of enemies during a battle. I became the Moon Clan's Enforcer when I hunted down the bastards that killed First Son's Mother. It was as if the Dark Consort took over my body. I did not care who I killed, as long as they were the enemy. I don't remember much of those I killed or even the kills themselves. First Son said that you had the same look of death in your eyes yesterday as I did that day. It is my job to get blood on my hands, so the rest of the Clan's can stay clean." He looked at me. "Out of the humans you killed, how many were for the sheer pleasure of it?" I started to answer with all of them, but he cut me off saying, "Without you doing it to defend or avenge someone?"

I held up a zero.

He gazed into the fire, a contemplative look on his face. "I talked with the Elder, and with First Son's account, he has decided to change your position in the Clan. He wants me to train you to be my Second Enforcer. We need to kill without hesitation, and after what we saw, the Elder believes that it would be the better path for you. It will be harder than anything you have done here so far. You will have to become an expert in all weapons and hand to hand combat. Do you accept? By accepting, you will be training under me more, and you will have to take the test to become my Second. If you become my Second, if there's a battle to be had, we are the first and last on the field."

I took my time to make my decision. I would not be protecting the village like I initially thought. Would it be the better fit? The Elder seemed to think so. I liked sparring with Howling Wolf, but something told me that this would be much different. I looked into his dark eyes and nodded. I was not sure what emotion crossed his face, but it was not one of his normal ones. Maybe it was worry and regret?

"Get to sleep. We start tomorrow at dawn."

Chapter 09

Howling Wolf slammed me into the dirt, knocking the wind from my lungs. "Get up," he commanded from above me.

I was tired, but I did not wait for him to say it again. I learned the hard way a while ago that he would kick me while I was down. I rolled to the side as his heel came down where my stomach was.

The Snow Cat prowled at the edge of my mind, waiting to be released. The last time she fought for me, he knocked us out. Every time I tried to use her, he would knock us out. He refused to let me use her, wanting to strengthen my abilities without her. When he felt comfortable that I could do well without her, he promised that he would let her play.

I rolled back up to standing. Sweat dripped down my skin, and I had to wipe it away before it got into my eyes. I was only wearing light linen clothes. He was shirtless, only wearing pants. I could see the sweat on his chest as he came for me again. He punched and I blocked, but his other fist came around and slammed into my chest. I coughed up blood, falling to the ground. I could not find my breath as his foot came up to smash into my face. I blocked it with both of my arms at the last second, the pain vibrating through my muscles and bones.

Even after all I have learned from him, I felt like I was still on the first day. We had been working for over two years now, and we just arrived at the start of spring. We always started with a long run, wearing down the stores of energy I had. Next, was sparring. Followed by breakfast, weapons work, lunch, and learning something new and getting clean before dinner.

I just got my breaths back when he picked me up and flung me over his shoulder. I dropped to a roll and popped back up. I did not lash out at him, since today was a defense day. My goal was to just take what he gave and try not getting knocked out completely. He grabbed me and tried to throw me down, but I dropped my knee, pulling him over my shoulder instead. He stared at me from the ground, surprise on his face. It was only for an instant before he popped back up.

He got in close and punched me. I blocked each of the punches using alternating arms. He once hit me in the solar plexus because I used both arms to block just the one punch. I would not make that mistake again. I could feel the new bruises on top of the older ones, which just made my arms numb.

"Are you just going to defend? Or are you going to hit me?" He growled through his attacks. It was the first time that it would be a full sparring session.

I dropped to the ground, sweeping my leg at the backs of his knees, forcing them to bend forward. He fell on top of me, and we grappled.

I kicked out with my feet, keeping a firm grip on his wrists. He flipped over me, and I used the momentum to land on top of him. Then, I moved up to sit on his chest, moving so my legs were off to one side, preventing him from taking a full breath. I grabbed one of his arms, pulling it with me as I leaned back to his side. I kept hold of his arm, using my legs as leverage. Pain covered on his face, knowing that if I kept it up, it would dislocate his arm from the shoulder.

First Son called out to the two of us. "Time!"

I dropped his arm, releasing him from the pain. I stayed laying on my back, trying to will my aching body to stand up.

He rolled from under me, pulling me up. He helped me walk over to where the First Son was sitting, a bucket of water to help us cool down. "When did you learn to roll me over your shoulder?" Howling Wolf asked as he handed me a wet towel.

I grinned, not wanting to tell him that I learned it from before I ran from the cities. City Elves had their own methods of combat, usually fighting dirty, since sometimes that is the only way to win. I had been waiting for him to teach it to me, but I just did it without thinking.

"Starting tomorrow, you will both attack and defend, putting together everything you have learned."

I nodded as I ran the wet cloth over my overly hot skin. I hoped the cool spring air would give us a breeze to cool down.

Sparrow came over with breakfast. She set the food on the table and then looked at me. She carefully touched my face, moving to see the extent of the damage. "Do you have to be so rough with her, Wolf?"

"Yes, I have to be. She knew what she was getting into." He looked in my direction, but he cringed, seeing the damage he caused.

I waved him off, letting him know not to worry about it.

"Is she at least getting better?" she asked.

Thinking about how I was still getting pounded into the dirt, I shook my head.

"She is. She does not have the power that I do, but she makes up for it in speed. Sometimes, she is a blur when she is focused. If she has a dagger in her hands, she can easily cause a lot of damage before the enemy knows what hit them."

"She disagrees that she is getting better," Sparrow pointed out.

He caught my gaze. "Why don't you agree?"

I rolled my sleeves up, held up my arms, showing the mass of bruises. He just looked at them. I guess he did not realize what I was hiding under my sleeves.

"I am sorry, Snow." He looked like he hated the bruising, but I waved him off again. I had agreed to this and knew that there would be pain involved by sparring with him.

First Son sucked in a breath, seeing the dark purple mixing with the green. "Not going to lie, I am glad that I am not you."

I smirked, thinking that he could not handle being me on my best days, much less the painful ones.

"So, how much longer do you think she has?" he asked, while Sparrow pushed food in front of me to eat.

"If she keeps it up, she could test at the end of the planting season," Howling Wolf replied. The test was going to be a no-holds back, no time limit spar with the warriors then him. "How is your own work coming?" he asked First Son.

"We are getting better at working as a team, but we keep hitting little snags," First Son admitted. He and his friends had become warriors after the Gauntlet, but they were technically still in training, just getting better while the Clan was at peace. I learned that warriors never really stopped training and kept working on perfecting themselves.

We finished eating, Sparrow taking First Son with her until lunch. I went with Howling Wolf and today, we were working with the bow, since that was still my weakest weapon. I was much better at close contact weapons, like my dagger and spear. We learned that I fought better with two daggers, instead of one. He set up the targets before we started.

My arms were shaking as I drew the bowstring back. I let loose the arrow, and it hit the top edge of the target, just missing it.

He came up behind me. "You are still too high." He laid his chin on my shoulder and re-aimed the bow. "Try here." He helped me pull the string back, letting me get the feel of it, without relying on my shaky arms. We let the string go at the same time, the arrow hitting dead center of the target.

"I know your arms hurt, and that is affecting your aiming. But as Enforcers, we do not get the luxury of slowing down when we are in pain," he explained right next to my ear. "If it was anyone else, I would have suggested stopping after the first few weeks. But I know that you can handle this and anything else that I can throw at you." He moved away from me, handing me another arrow.

I set it in the notch to aim it. I closed my eyes and took a deep breath, pushing the pain in my arms down as far as I could. A moment later, I opened my eyes and raised the bow. I drew the string back, taking another deep breath as I aimed. The arrow flew, hitting closer to the center of the target that I had before.

He picked me up and twirled me. "Yes!" He realized what he did and set me back on the ground. "Sorry about that. It is just that once you have this down, the only thing left is sparring with me. We might be able to test you earlier than I originally thought." He grinned, "Or maybe I will take the extra time to let your Snow Cat try to beat me. Since I am sure she is raring for a fight." My answer to him was giving him the hiss the Snow Cat wanted to give him. "Such a snarly pair of cats." He pointed back to the target, a silent command to keep working.

Chapter 10

"Honorable Elder, I believe Silent Snow is ready for her test of abilities. I have taught her everything I know, and she has become an expert in all of our weapons," Howling Wolf announced in front of the Clan one morning before the sun rose.

The Elder looked down, then called out to the Clan, "Does anyone second his recommendation to test Silent Snow?"

First Son stood up and stepped forward. "Honorable Elder, I second the recommendation."

"By seconding the recommendation, you understand that you will be putting your life and the lives of your fellow warriors in her hands."

"I understand, Honorable Elder. I stand by my words."

"Is there anyone who refutes these two?" No one said a word, so he looked to me, "What say you, Silent Snow? Are you willing to put the lives of other warriors in your hands, knowing should you fail, their lives can perish?"

I used my hands to tell them that I deferred to the two warriors.

"Then I grant permission to test you." He looked back to the Clan. "The test will start at dawn."

Howling Wolf and the First Son escorted me to where the test would take place. Sparrow came running over. "Are you sure about this, Wolf?"

"I am positive. The test has two parts. The first half, you will compete against the other warriors, those who are considered experts in their weapons. You must beat them all in a contest of accuracy. Then, you will spar with every warrior in the Clan, then you will take me on."

I swallowed hard, trying to see if I would be able to do what he was asking of me. Why did I defer to him?

"It is all right. If I did not think you were ready, I would not have recommended the test today. For the accuracy, just take a deep breath. For the sparring, do not use the Snow Cat unless you must. But I will let her dance with me when you get to me. I want you to fight with everything you have. Got the weapons for her?"

Sparrow pulled out a pair of fake knives, covered in an oily paint. "These should feel the same as your dagger. Since you will not be using real weapons on our warriors, these will work. You just must use them like your regular dagger. If the warriors are hit with what is considered a killing blow, they are out. But the same is true for you. If they get a killing blow on you, you fail the test."

I grabbed the fake knives, feeling their weight and balance. She was right. They felt exactly like my dagger. We had worked with two for the training, but it would not be realistic outside of training.

Howling Wolf saw my confusion before he pulled out a dagger from the sheath under his shirt. "I found your dagger's partner. I knew that you would need it after seeing you fight with two of them. But you only get it if you take it from me," he bribed.

The other warriors came into the arena, stripping off most of their clothes, leaving only their lower underwear on. I followed suit and stripped down to only the binding wrap and my own underwear. The women set up everything, so we all could conserve our strength. They came over to give me good luck touches. They would not go easy on me, because they needed to know that I could keep them alive. I was just happy that they saw me as one of them. The Elder and Grandfather sat at the top of the arena, able to watch everything.

Xerinae called to them, "Honorable Elder and Honorable Grandfather, the arena is set for the testing of Silent Snow."

"Then we begin!" the Elder called out.

The first weapon test was the bow and arrow. I was glad that I had finally gotten the hang of the stupid contraption.

The other warrior shook my hand, before he took his shots. Three arrows, each close to the bullseye. He passed the bow to me. I closed my eyes and took a deep breath. I opened them and grabbed the arrow from the quiver next to us. I knocked the arrow, took careful aim, and let it loose. The first shot went to the outside of his arrows. My stomach dropped, but I refused to give up. I shot my second one, just inside of his. I would need a bullseye to beat him in points.

I took one last deep breath and grabbed the arrow. I thought I could feel Howling Wolf at my back, as I thought about the first time, I hit the target. I released the arrow, hoping that it would not be my last test. I heard cheers as I looked to see that I made it just inside the bullseye. I sighed of relief as I handed the bow back to the archer.

One weapon down, three left. Next was the spear, which I felt comfortable with. The spearman handed me a spear, as he grabbed his. There were a pair of dummy targets set up with a bullseye on their chests. He went first, sprinting and stabbing as he lunged. The spear hit inside the bullseye. He came back towards me. I held the spear differently than him, using two hands to steady it. I ran forward and lunged, hitting inside the bullseye as well. I could not tell who won this one, so Xerinae came down to measure the distances from the spear tips to the center. She measured three times, just to be sure.

"Silent Snow is closer by almost half an inch, Honorable Elder."

The spearman shook my hand, accepting her ruling.

Halfway done. The axe man smiled as he picked up the axe. He threw three of them, hitting the targets with good accuracy. I threw mine, hitting just inside of his all three times. We shook hands, before he retrieved the axes.

One weapon left and it was the one I was best at. I grabbed the dagger at my hip, before meeting with the next champion. We were each given one slash to cause the dummy to die of 'blood loss'. He slashed the dummy's throat, leaving a gaping gash on its neck. I stepped forward, seeing a slaver's face on the dummy. I spun around, slashing with my dagger using my rage and hatred to fuel the weapon.

When I finished facing away from the dummy, I glanced over at the champion. His eyes were wide, so I turned to look. The dummy's head was hanging by a few threads. A flash of embarrassment wafted through me, until I saw the look of pride in Howling Wolf's eyes.

I put the dagger back into its sheath and gave it to Sparrow. She handed me the twin fake knives. This was close hand combat between the other warriors and I, before Howling Wolf and I would spar hand-to-hand. I stood in the center of all of them, as if I had gotten behind enemy lines and was surrounded. They each had versions of their weapons like I had, paint covered facsimiles of their favorite weapons. I took a deep breath and stood in my ready stance.

"Begin!" the Elder commanded.

The warriors came at me from all sides. The thrum of bow strings announced the flight of arrows. I ducked down, letting the arrows hit some of the other warriors. I knew that even as confident as I was in my daggers and myself, I would not have been able to defeat them without thinning their numbers a little. Those who were hit with what were considered killing blows left the field.

I swung around, the fake knives' hilts leaning against my arms, reinforcing them. I hit a few of them in the neck or face, calling them out. Then I ducked under someone using a spear and slashed up to call him out as well. I felt them hit me a few times, but nothing that would cause any real damage, even if they were real weapons. Someone grabbed me from behind, so I tossed one of the fake knives up, caught it blade down. I stabbed backward, hitting him in the stomach. He dropped me, and I swung up at the person who was going to kill me while the warrior held me.

Soon, it was down to a few warriors and me, all of us out of breath. My muscles ached and burned, but I pushed the pain down, awakening the Snow Cat. I kept her ready but did not want her to come out yet. I waited for them to come at me, standing in a defensive position. When the bowstring thrummed, I blocked it, I knocked the arrow away from me with one of the fake knives. I threw one of the knives and tapped him in the chest.

I was down to one knife, so the last three attacked. My foot touched a spear, so I put my foot under it to pop the spear up into my hands. I stabbed toward one of them and got him. But another warrior came to my side. I blocked his axe with the fake knife, then pulled the spear back to slam into his stomach. I cut him across the neck as he fell back, his breath knocked from him.

It was down to one warrior and me. First Son and I circled one another. We each hoped our opponent would drop their guard. He had a pair of smaller axes, matching the fake knives that he saw me use together. I blinked, the familiar blue tint taking over. I hissed at him.

He smiled before he attacked. He raised the first axe to come down on me, but I blocked it with the spear. He came around to slam the axe into my midsection, but I blocked it with my last knife. He pushed down and up at the same time with his two different axes. He was a lot stronger than me, and I bet that he had a lot more energy as well.

I thought about a move one of the City Elves taught me a long time ago. It was a risk, but if I did not do something, he would overpower me. I dropped the guard on the spear, letting the axe come down, I moved out of the way just before it hit me. He lost his balance, dropping the attack on my knife. I used the knife to slash at his artery. He was out.

I looked to make sure there was no one else, before Howling Wolf came for me. I dropped the weapons and stood ready for him. He stopped just in front of me, sending a testing kick. I blocked it with one arm, when I saw his fist heading toward me. I ducked, going under his arm to uppercut him. It was only a glancing blow, so he easily withstood it. He was right that my speed would have to be my advantage. He swept his foot, forcing me to jump, but he popped up and tackled me to the ground.

"Play with me, Kitty Cat." He punched me, splitting my lip open.

I put my feet in his pelvis, kicking him over me. I tried to keep a hold of his arm, but the sweat from before made me slippery. I wondered if I could use that as an advantage. He slid to a stop, then launched himself back at me as I was standing back up. I touched his shoulders and leapfrogged over him as he passed under me. I landed on all fours, whipping around as he rolled and kicked himself back to standing.

We circled, both trying to find that one weak spot that would end the fight. He came at me, a flurry of punches. I blocked them as fast as I could. I just needed one weakness to get through to him. I slammed my heel into his toes, and as he fell back, I elbowed him in the face. Blood hit the two of us, as he backed away. He looked either impressed or pissed, but I was not sure which.

Once his vision cleared, he grabbed me, pulling me into his arms, wrapping his other arm around my neck. Blood dripped on my shoulder, and I remembered that I was slippery from sweat. I pulled my arm from his hand and used both elbows to aim for his ribs. I threw everything I had into it, knowing that if he did not let go, I would lose consciousness. He dropped me, the pain in his ribs too much to hold me. I whipped around to face him. I grabbed his head and helped him to become acquainted with my knee. He fell back, so I grabbed him and threw him forward.

I dropped to the ground; my energy completely gone. The Snow Cat fell back into her den, tired from the fight. I glanced to Howling Wolf, staring at the blood on his face. I did not mean to hit him that hard.

"The test is complete! Silent Snow has passed!" the Elder announced.

I looked around to see that I was still in the arena. I forgot that Howling Wolf and I were not just sparring normally. I grimaced as he sat up, pressing his hand to his face.

Sparrow came running over and put a cold cloth to his face. She worked on the blood splatter. I reached forward to touch him, but Sparrow whacked my hand away. "Do not touch him. Not until you are cleaned up. We do not want to introduce more germs to his wound."

Howling Wolf grabbed my hand in his. "It is all right, Snow." He sounded like he was in pain, and it hurt me to know that I was the one who caused it.

Hot tears streamed down my cheeks, mad at myself for hurting him, mad at him for letting me.

First Son came over to help me stand, "Why is she crying? Are you hurt?"

I shook my head, because physically, I was all right. I then pointed to Howling Wolf and said hurt with my hands.

"You are crying because you hurt him?"

I nodded.

"You did not cry for hurting me," he mumbled to himself.

"You are not on the ground bleeding. That is why she did not cry over you," Sparrow said matter-of-factly. "Now, be careful, because it's just a quick patch job." She faced me. "I need to fix your lip."

I shook my head, putting my hand in front of it. I made Howling Wolf bleed, so it only made sense that I bled as well.

"Sometimes I hate that all of my friends are warriors."

"Two of them are Enforcers," First Son pointed out.

"I know," she snapped. "That is even worse than regular warriors." She helped Howling Wolf stand up. "Now I have double the work when something happens."

The warriors came around us, now that Howling Wolf was back to on his feet. They kept touching my shoulders and head, since I was shorter than all of them. They said their congratulations to me, and then a few teased Howling Wolf about how I broke his face.

He just told them in a solemn voice, "I forgot that she is wily. But if any of you want to see how hard she hits, I will let her spar you one on one."

I wiped the blood from my lip, feeling the burning of the sweat getting into it. They kept talking, while I escaped toward the river and its spring.

I made it to the spring with no one following me. I took off the last of my clothes and dove into the cool water. It felt great on my skin as I splashed in the water. I cleaned the binding wrap and underwear, setting them on a rock to dry. I scrubbed my skin with the sand and cleaned the cut on my lip.

"Mind if I join you?"

I glanced up to see Howling Wolf sitting on the shore.

I splashed him in answer.

He took off his own underwater, set down the clothes he was holding, and dove into next to me. He popped back out of the water, splashing me back. This began a water war between us. He grabbed me and tossed me into the air, where I hit the water with a big splash. After a while, we both pulled ourselves back into the shoreline. His face did not look as bad as I thought it was going to, since he cleaned the blood off.

He turned to face me, while I stared at the stars coming out. "You should really let Sparrow take care of your lip. I did not think you would not move to block me when I punched you."

I looked at him, then shook my head. I lightly touched his skin where I split his cheek.

"You are refusing help with your lip because you made me bleed?"

I nodded.

"Yet, I am the one who hurt you first."

I shrugged.

He moved closer to me, our heads close, bodies pointed opposite ways. "I know it is not polite to ask, but is there anyone who is missing you in the cities?"

I asked him if he meant a family.

"Family, friends, a lover?"

110

I laughed silently, as I shook my head. Then I used my hands to explain that other City Elves feared me because they all thought I was cursed.

"Cursed? How so?"

I told him that it was because I constantly rebelled where I could. The other City Elves did not want anything to do with me, because they worried that they would be punished for my wrongdoing. None of them realized that I chose to be punished for theirs.

He stayed silent for a time, and we stared at the stars above. "Since you missed it the past two years because you were training with me, the after the planting season is considered the season when eligible males and females try to see if they can catch the eye of the Elf they want to be with."

I made a bird with my hands, asking about Sparrow.

"She is one of those eligible women."

I asked about First Son.

"He is also eligible. Why do you ask?"

I made a bird, crossed my fingers, then for First Son.

Howling Wolf coughed. "You think they would be good together?"

I nodded.

111

"Who would you set up with me?" He asked coyly.

I thought about it and made the symbol for Xerinae.

He choked. "Please, tell me you are kidding."

I shook my head. I told him about the gossip girls and how they keep talking about him and how they want to... I stopped signing, trying to figure out a way to say that they wanted his babies. I just gave him the symbol for children and hoped he understood.

He smacked his hand to his forehead. "Oh, Goddess Above." I pat his upper arm sympathetically. "What about you? Whose eye are you going to try to catch?" He leaned over me as I made a face and laughed. "What is that face for?"

I explained how the gossip girls kept trying to get eligible warriors to be with me by encouraging any interest someone showed of me.

"I did not know about that. None of the warriors said anything about that."

I shrugged. I told him that I was not trying to catch anyone's eye, and I just wanted to enjoy my freedom.

"Well, I think there is someone out there who is bound to get your attention." He laid back down.

I looked over at him, before sitting up. I asked him why he was asking me about this.

"Because you are something different than the rest of us. More than just your silver hair, scars, and the fact that you are a City Elf. So, I wondered if you had thought about having someone to spend your life with." He sat up and put his back to mine. "Elves live for almost ten thousand years, so it can become a lonely existence sometimes. Since you are not able to communicate clearly, I wonder if it is worse for you." He turned his head up towards the sky, leaning back on my shoulder. "I just want you to have the kind of life you want to have."

I held my hands over his sightline. I told him that I already had the life I have been dreaming about. Truthfully, the only thing that would make it better was if we could liberate all the City Elves from their slavery. But that was beyond a hopeless dream.

"That reminds me!" He stood up and grabbed something from the pile of clothes. He came back over to me and helped me stand up. "I owe you something." He handed me the two daggers, mine, and its partner. "For beating me." He also handed me a new sheath that would hold each dagger on both sides of my hips.

My fingertips felt something embroidered on the sheath, but I could not see it in the dying light. I tried to shift it in the light to see it better, but he lowered my hands, looking a little bit embarrassed.

"Do not look at the designs until later."

I nodded, holding the sheaths and daggers close to me.

"We should probably get back to the village now."

I grabbed my now dry binding wrap and underwear and put them on. I dressed in the black linen dress that he handed me, covering the bruises from the test.

He walked me back to Sparrow's house since I still did not have one of my own. I stepped inside and faced him. I touched his uninjured cheek, mouthing 'thank you.'

He kissed my palm and walked away.

In the light from the candles, I looked at the shining thread on the sheaths. On one of them was an image of a Snow Cat; on the other sheath was the image of a Wolf. I smiled to myself, wondering if he had been trying to catch my eye, and I just did not know it.

Chapter 11

First Son knocked on the door, waking me up. He had a different kind of knock that Howling Wolf or any of the gossip girls. Letting Sparrow sleep some more, I walked over and opened the door. "The Elder needs to see us."

I looked past him to see Howling Wolf running toward the house. I yawned, before telling them one minute. I went back inside and changed into my black linen gear, matching what Howling Wolf wore. I placed the daggers in their sheaths on my hips, then put on the black boots Xerinae made me after my test. Then I quietly stepped out from the house to face them and gave them a thumbs up.

"Did the Elder say why he needed to see us?" Howling Wolf asked as he walked toward the large building where he and Grandfather lived.

Since my Enforcer test, First Son had become the highest-ranking warrior, moving quickly through the ranks. "No, he did not. I know that a messenger came before dawn and dropped a letter at the message stone." The message stones were a way for the different Clans to communicate without stepping into each other's lands. Sometimes those stones were the only way that peace was kept between the Clans. I wondered what this one could say that would require the three of us. I concluded that nothing good comes from things that happen before dawn.

We entered the large building to see the Elder and Grandfather sitting in front of the fire.

"Honorable Elder, how can we be of assistance?" Howling Wolf asked, the three of us bowing our heads.

"First Son told you that there was a message left on the message stone?" he asked, handing the letter to Howling Wolf.

I tried to read their faces, but all I saw was anger. I waited until the two tall males were done reading, before they handed the letter to me.

It was a challenge to our Clan. It demanded that we send our best fighter to fight their own in a battle to the death. The fighter was to come alone. If we refused, they would attack our village. If we sent a fighter and they died, they would not attack us. I narrowed my eyes at the letter, knowing that Howling Wolf or First Son would try to go to face this battle. First Son and Sparrow were just now learning they wanted to catch each other's eyes and hearts. Howling Wolf would try to go, but Sparrow would be sad if he did not make it back. I handed the letter back to the Elder, watching him put it in an easily accessible pocket.

"Who sent it?" First Son asked the Elder.

"The Star Clan." Grandfather pulled out a map of the Clans, pointing to where their village was.

"Why would they challenge us?" First Son asked.

"We should be under the assumption that it is a challenge for dominance in the region." The Elder looked at me. "Silent Snow, when you first came here, you told Grandfather and I that the Moon Clan is known to the City Elves. Have you heard of the Star Clan?"

I shook my head, only the Moon Clan being the threat to City Elves if we tried to escape into the forests.

"My guess would be that they want to be feared as we are."

"How are we going to respond?" Howling Wolf asked. "If we ignore it, they will attack the village. If we send someone, they will probably kill them, since this could just be a trap to kill one of our warriors."

I kept my eyes on the map, memorizing it.

Grandfather caught me staring and rolled up the map. "What do you think, Silent Snow?"

117

I used my hands to tell them that I agreed with Howling Wolf's assessment. What kind of a Clan would let an enemy walk right in, kill their top fighter, then let them leave? If it is a trap, then would we be willing to sacrifice one of our own to save the rest of the Clan? I asked them how many they thought Star Clan had in warriors.

"From the reports I've read, they have about three times as many warriors as we do." So, if we made them come to us, there was a very good chance that our Clan would die. And if we brought every warrior with us, there would not be any left to protect the village.

Howling Wolf and First Son must have had the same thoughts I did, because First Son asked, "Do the lives of the many outweigh the life of one?"

"That is what we have to decide and choose," The Elder said, voice hushed.

As Enforcers, Howling Wolf and I would be the first choices, but since I was his Second, he would go at the drop of a hat. It would not matter if it was a trap, as long as he protected the Clan with his life, that is all that mattered to him.

"When do we have to decide by?" Howling Wolf asked them.

"Letter says three days. Add in travel time, and we need to decide by morning."

"We will all think about this and reconvene tonight?" First Son suggested.

We all agreed, and the Elder walked us out, letting us think on our own. I knew each of us would volunteer to go, giving up our lives for the Clan. I climbed onto Sparrow's house, letting the height give me a better perspective. I would have to wait until no one noticed me gone. I fell asleep, planning on leaving after dusk.

"Snow?" Howling Wolf climbed onto the roof with me.

I opened my eyes and gazed at his dark ones.

He sat next to me and asked, "Have you thought about what we should do?"

I shook my head, signing that I still did not know what the right answer was. I then thought of an idea, though it would require help. I just had to hope I could convince Raven to help me. I asked Howling Wolf what time it was.

He looked at the sun. "You missed breakfast and lunch. Dinner is about to be served."

I yawned and stretched. My stomach grumbled at the lack of food, and Howling Wolf laughed.

119

"Let us get you some dinner. We will need our strength to figure this out." We climbed off the roof and went into the dining building.

I caught Raven's eyes, and he nodded to me. I excused myself from the table with Howling Wolf, Sparrow, and First Son.

Raven met me in the kitchen area and asked, "What is going on, Snow?"

I explained that I was not sleeping well, and I wondered if I could borrow some of the sleeping poison to help me sleep.

"I do not know, Snow..."

I gave him my best smile, putting my hands on his shoulders. Then I pulled one hand away to tell him that it is for the best, and that if needed, he could just blame me for it. He handed me the little pouch he had in his inner pocket.

"Just a sprinkle should help you sleep tonight. Any more than that, and you will be out for a couple of days."

I mimed just a sprinkle, so he felt better about letting me borrow it. I tucked it into my shirt and gave him a hug as a thank you. Then I went back to the table, and they were discussing the letter. I listened as they all tried to figure out what to do. After dinner, we left Sparrow and went back to the large building. Grandfather was about to make some tea, but I volunteered to do it for him, since I still did not have any ideas. He thanked me, leaving me in the kitchen. I slipped the sleeping poison in all the cups, including my own. After pouring the tea, I carried the cups to the males, leaving mine in the kitchen.

First Son and Howling Wolf were arguing over which one of them would go, since that was the only plan, they came up with. I went back to the kitchen and grabbed my own cup. When I came back into the main room, only Howling Wolf was fighting off the sleeping poison, the other three already asleep.

"Why, Snow?" he asked as he fell further into the chair.

I gave him a sad smile before signing to him that he is too important to lose.

I kissed his forehead as he fell asleep. I grabbed the map and the letter from the Elder. I left a note telling them that I was sorry for poisoning them, but this was the best idea I had to keep my friends and Clan safe. I thanked them for everything that they gave me, so giving my life to save them was worth it.

I took my Snow Cat cloak and headed toward the Star Clan, using the night vision of the Snow Cat spirit to guide my way.

Chapter 12

As soon as I crossed into the border to the Star Clan's land, I held the letter in my hands, just in case I was stopped. I did not find anyone until I reached their village, as marked on the map. I was glad I decided to rest on the Moon Clan's land before coming here. It was dawn and when I arrived in their village, the Snow Cat and I were fully rested.

A scout spotted me and yelled that there was an intruder.

I held up the letter for them to see, keeping my hands away from the daggers at my hips.

More warriors came out to attack me but stopped before they got too close. One of them grabbed the letter from my hand and read it. He motioned for them to escort me to the village Elder.

"What is the meaning of this?" their Elder demanded in the Common language when he saw me.

"She is the answer to our challenge, Elder," the warrior that held the letter told him.

"Does the Moon Clan think we are fools?!" he yelled.

I shook my head.

"Then why would they send a City Elf woman here?" He leaned in close to me.

I tried to answer with my hands, but the warriors thought I was getting too close to my weapons.

"Why do you not speak?"

I mimed that I could not.

"Goddess Above, they sent us a sacrifice instead of a fighter."

I thumbed to myself and put my fists up to show that I was a fighter. "You? A fighter? Is the Moon Clan's reputation just talk?" I bared my teeth. I pointed to the letter then to the Champion, who I pinned as their strongest. I motioned that I would beat him.

"We should send our warriors to destroy the Moon Clan if they claim that she is their best fighter."

The Champion stared at me before he asked, "Are you claiming to be their strongest fighter?"

I nodded.

"If they sent you as a proxy, we will kill you and your Clan. If you are their strongest fighter and you lose, you will die, leaving your Clan alone. Do you agree to the terms?"

I smiled, putting my hand out to shake on it.

He shook it, turning to the Elder. "Something is strange about her. Why would they have a City Elf in the first place? And why is she wearing the pelt of a Snow Cat? If she killed it, then we are underestimating her."

I just gave him an innocent smile and toyed with the ends of my braid.

"But if she was sent as a sacrifice, I doubt they would care if she died or not. Either way, it will warm me up for the morning."

He was confident, and I could use that. They led me to an interior arena, where their Clan gathered. The Elder stepped in front of his Clan, while I removed the Snow Cat cloak and the long-sleeved black tunic, showing them the many scars that adorned my skin. I could hear the Champion suck in breath, seeing them. Maybe he would underestimate me more, so that I had a chance to win. Even if I died during the battle, it would buy my Clan's freedom. I took off the long pants, leaving me in only the binding wrap and underwear, with my daggers at my hips. The Champion followed my lead, going down to his bottoms.

"This is the challenger?" I heard the crowd mumble, before someone shouted that this was unacceptable.

The Elder's voice was clear to his people. "She has agreed that if she is killed too soon, that we would go after her Clan. If she believes and proves that she is a strong warrior, we will give her a warrior's death and keep our oath." He turned to face the warrior and me. "If the two of you are ready..."

I nodded to him, before turning to my opponent. Then I grabbed my daggers and stood in my defensive position.

The Champion grabbed his own two-handed axe, standing ready.

"Begin!" The Elder shouted.

I waited for him, as he raised his axe toward me, using both hands to grip it. He rushed me, faster than I anticipated. He swung the axe downward, and I crossed my arms to catch under the blade. He pressed down hard, but I kicked him in the stomach, pushing him away from me. I ducked under the axe as it fell to the wayside.

He kept his grip on it with one hand, trying to catch his breath. Realization filled his eyes as he understood he underestimated me, so I needed to finish this quickly.

I rushed at him; daggers ready to slice into his flesh. He used the handle and the blade of the axe to block me, moving it up and down to push my arms out of the way. He pushed me back with the length of the axe handle. He came toward me, swinging low. I moved back, watching him switch his grip. I caught the axe on its upswing with the daggers crossing over the base of the blade at my side. He let go of the axe and punched me in the face. I jumped back just before he connected, but he still caught me in the cheek.

Blood ran from the side of my mouth. I wiped it away, letting the Snow Cat take over. Her vision tinted mine. I went after him, striking as fast as I could. He kept trying to block it, but my agility was too fast for him. He tried to swing the axe up to hit me in the chin with the blade, but I slammed one of the daggers between the blade and the hilt, the opening just big enough for my dagger. I tossed the other dagger to the ground and twisted the dagger trapped in the axe's weak point. I did not care that I cut my hand. I ripped the axe from his grip and sent the axe flying away from us.

The clan members mumbled, proving that I was a fighter like they hoped for. He tackled me to the ground, trying to grab at the dagger to rip it away from me.

I pulled my knees to my chest, before kicking him in the ribs over me. I used that momentum to land on top of him, like I did Howling Wolf during one of the times we sparred. I moved to put my knees in his shoulders, ready to jam the dagger into his throat. He caught my hand with his crossed wrists, trying to grab onto hands without letting the dagger slip. I used my other hand to reinforce my strength, putting my weight into it. Someone in the crowd sobbed, and the Snow Cat retreated into her den, leaving me to choose whether I would kill him or not. His wrists slipped, the sweat from the fight making his skin slick. Another woman cried out as I jammed the dagger into the ground next to his throat.

His eyes were wide, as I ripped the dagger from the dirt and grabbed my other one.

I got off him, standing up. I sheathed my daggers, and no one moved.

"Mercy? You are giving him mercy?" the Elder asked in disbelief.

I looked to the Champion as he struggled to get up, his breathing ragged from when I slammed him into the ground. I nodded to the Elder and walked to the Champion, putting my hand near him, to help him stand if he chose. He chose to grab it and pull me back down, moving his body over mine. I grabbed the daggers, sliding them from their sheaths just before he reached for my throat. I slashed at his arms, his blood hitting my face. He let me go, sat back, and howled in pain.

I returned to my feet and wiped the blood from the daggers, putting one away. I shot a look at the Elder, telling him to call it my win. He refused, so I allowed the Snow Cat take back over as I walked over the injured man. I grabbed his hair, exposing his neck to the Clan, set the blade against his throat, and waited. He did not move, not wanting to test if I would kill him. Then I looked to the Clan and saw the woman who was weeping. My gaze shifted from her to the Elder, and then back to her. I removed the knife from his throat and slammed my knee in his temple instead, knocking him unconscious.

I stepped toward the Elder, waiting for him to decide if his Champion would live or die. I looked to the woman who was crying and motioned for her to go to the Champion, putting the second dagger away as a sign of good faith.

She ran from where the Clan was watching over to the Champion.

I took off the binding wrap, using one of the daggers to cut it in half, and handed it to her to stop his bleeding.

She looked to the wrap, to me, then to the Elder. "Father, stop this!" she pleaded as she took the wraps to stop the man from bleeding from the arm wounds.

The Elder stepped up to me, but I gave him no indication that I would back down. "You could have killed him, but you chose not to. Why?" he asked, his voice weak and close to silent.

I pointed to the woman, then mimed that I heard her crying.

"You did not kill him, because my daughter was crying for him?"

I nodded, the Snow Cat receding again, the fight over.

The Elder raised my hand over my head and said, "The challenger has won and graciously shown our Champion mercy." He let my arm go. "I do not understand how you were able to defeat him or how you moved so quickly. You are truly a warrior, and I understand why the Moon Clan sent you."

I grinned and dressed. I was not sure how to explain that they did not send me, but since he could not read my hand speaking, there was no point in trying.

The woman struggled to pick the Champion up, so I ran over to help her carry him. She nodded and said, "We will take him to the Healing House."

I followed her lead, waiting for the Clan to decide what they were going to do. Since I gave their Champion mercy, if they had any honor, they would not attack me. I prayed to the Goddess Above that they had honor, as I carried the Champion to where the woman designated. She let go of him to open the door, and my strength started to fail. We hurried to get him into a bed before I fell to the side away from it.

An older woman came into the Healing House and looked at the Champion then me. I pointed to the warrior, so she would get him fixed up. The older woman told the younger one to get herbs and clean water. I watched and waited to make sure the Champion would be all right.

The younger woman knelt to me and handed me a cup of clear water. I sniffed it.

"You let him live. I am not going to repay that kindness with poison," she growled before her face softened. "Thank you for not killing him."

I lifted the cup to her, giving her a "you are welcome" salute, then sipped the water.

The Elder came in and talked to the older woman, "Grandmother."

I jolted at her title. I guess that is what the Wood Elves called their healers.

"Will Ursus be all right?"

The old woman nodded. "He will need to sleep it off, but the wounds she gave him were shallow and had already started to clot when I got to him. She went for quick pain, not to actually harm him." The old woman looked down to me. "You are a strange woman, City Elf."

The younger woman helped me stand, then sit on the chair Grandmother told her to set me in. "Take this off." She pulled the shirt off and looked at the scars. "How does someone so young have so many scars?" she asked, running her hands along my shoulders, feeling the rippled skin under her fingertips.

"Since you can't speak, can you write?"

I nodded and made the gesture for writing, hoping she would have something.

The younger woman handed me a piece of chalk and a black piece of wood.

I wrote 'slavery' in the common language on it to answer the Grandmother's question.

She put the shirt back on me. I looked to the Elder, waiting for him to ask his questions. "We will start simple. What is your name?"

'Silent Snow.'

"Why do your eyes change colors?"

'Snow Cat spirit in me.'

I could see the wheels in his head turning until he asked the question that he was ready to ask. "We were not expecting you to win, nor were we expecting mercy, so I've decided to give you a boon. What is it you want?"

I glanced at the ground, trying to figure out what would be the best for the Moon Clan. Then I wrote that I was not expecting to win, so I would like to request an alliance between Clans.

"You came here ready to die?" the young woman asked. She looked to the Elder, "This would be a boon for both Clans. If she is the strongest warrior, as an ally, she would come to our aid in our time of need."

I hesitated before writing, 'Not the strongest. Second strongest. Just fastest.'

The Elder, the Grandmother, and the young woman paled. "If they had sent their strongest..." the Elder mumbled to himself.

I wrote on the board, 'Not sent. Chose to come.'

"The Moon Clan is as the rumors stated then," the Grandmother spoke.

I nodded to them, as the warrior woke up.

I wrote on the board, 'Good morning, sunshine!' as a cheeky way to remind him of my victory.

He jumped when he saw me, before he saw the Elder and Grandmother. He then saw the younger woman's tears and calmed down. "What happened?"

"She bested you. And instead of killing you, she gave you mercy," the young woman told him and grabbed his hands in hers. "Her name is Silent Snow, and because she won, she has asked for an alliance with our Clan." She looked to the Elder and asked, "Are we going to give it to her?"

The Elder coughed and nodded. "As a boon for her and our Clan, we will accept her request."

My stomach grumbled, reminding me that I had not eaten anything since dinner a day and a half ago. My face burned red as I stared at the ground.

"Well, let us get them some food, so they can regain their strength." The Grandmother laughed. She looked to the warrior. "Think you will be able to walk?"

The Champion looked at me as I stood up. Not to be outdone, he tried to stand as well. He wobbled but held firm. As I took a step, he took one, too. By sheer force of wills, we both made it to the dining area of the village, before falling into the seats of the table. To make things easier, I kept a hold of the chalk and blackboard. I looked at the sky, the sun proclaiming it to be midday. The young woman went to get food for us, while the Champion and I just stared at each other. It was more of him glaring while I gave an innocent smile.

The young woman sat down as I wrote her a question about her name. "Oh, where are my manners? My name is Cristata, and this is Ursus."

Ursus asked me questions after that, starting with how I was so fast.

I wrote about the Snow Cat spirit and how her speed made me faster in my own right.

"Did your Clan give you those scars?" he growled. "What kind of Clan would harm one of their people like that? You must have centuries of them all over you-"

"Where is she?!" I shrank as Howling Wolf's voice boomed over the low rumble of the Star Clan talking. "Where is our City Elf?!"

Ursus looked to my reaction, then to where the voice was coming from. He stood up, using his anger to help him stand and stomp.

Cristata helped me stand up to get between them as Ursus yelled at Howling Wolf, the First Son, and the other warriors.

"How dare you come into our village and demand anything!" Ursus pushed Howling Wolf back. "What makes you think we are going to return her to people who tortured her body enough to have those kinds of scars?!"

I slid between them, stopping Ursus from pushing Wolf again. Then I shook my head at him, trying to stop the misunderstanding from becoming worse. I saw the Elder, flanked with his other warriors.

"You think we caused those?" First Son aske.

"Where else would she have gotten them? She has centuries worth, and since she is a part of your Clan, then you must have caused them!" Ursus yelled, as the Star Clan's warriors moved closer.

Howling Wolf pushed me to the side. "She was a slave for the humans for twenty-seven hundred years before she came to us! We would never harm one of our own like that! And who are you to keep our Clanswoman away from us?"

"How could you send her to be the challenger?" Ursus shot back. "She could have died, and you sent her instead of another warrior."

"We did not send her anywhere. She poisoned us with sleep poison, then took the letter and ran. We just now were able to catch up to her." Howling Wolf glared at me. "Since you are still alive, I have to assume that you are a hostage here."

I punched him in the arm, shaking my head. I hand-signed that I had won and in return for sparing their warrior, we would have an alliance with them. My hands flew quickly, only Howling Wolf and First Son understanding them.

First Son looked to the other Clan's Elder and asked, "Is it true?"

"You can understand that?" the Elder sounded surprised and a little impressed.

"Usually, she does not go that fast, but I got the gist of it." I pushed First Son closer to the Elder. "She won, and now we have an alliance?" First Son asked the Elder.

"Yes, that would be correct." The Elder looked at me, before the First Son. "I am assuming since she pushed you forward, you are the emissary for the Moon Clan?"

"I am the First Son of our Elder," First Son explained. "I am not an emissary, but she believes I could represent the Clan." He looked back to me then Howling Wolf. "He wants to yell at you."

I looked at Howling Wolf, watching him grind his teeth. I nodded to First Son, then made my way to the angry male.

He grabbed me by the arm and pulled me into a random building. "What in the Sevens Hells is wrong with you?" he started. I tried to explain, but he stopped me. "You poisoned your own Clansmen! You poisoned me! What would make you do such a thing? Why can you not see that your life is just as precious as the rest of the Clans'? You came here to die, did you not?" He growled, "Answer me, Silent Snow!"

I just stood there, not sure which question to answer first. Although I knew that I was in the right if he could not see it, then this thing was not going to work out. I tried to tell him that I was his Second, and if I was not willing to step forward into a fight, and if he would try to stop me every time, then what was the point of having me become an Enforcer? I stood up straighter before signing that I came here because I truly believed that my Clansmen were worth saving. If I had any thought that doing this would not solve anything, then I would not have come. We both knew that someone had to be sacrificed, and he was more important to the Clan than I was.

"You are just as important, Snow. That is what I am trying to get you to see. You risk your life because the humans made you think that you are worthless. I have spent the past few years trying to show you that you are greater than you believe yourself to be. If you cannot see that, then I failed." He turned toward the door. "I made you my Second because I truly believed that you would do what you could to defend the Clan. You need to understand that you are a part of the Clan as well. Sometimes, we need to protect you from yourself." He left, leaving me in the random building on formerly-enemy soil.

I walked out of the building as he talked to the other warriors. I looked to First Son who was heading into the large building with the Elder and Grandmother.

Ursus and Cristata were walking back to the dining area, Ursus limping as he moved.

I just stood there, knowing that I created the rift between Howling Wolf and me. I wondered to myself if there would be any way to fix it. Add in that I poisoned the Elder and Grandfather...

Maybe I should not go back to the Moon Clan's village. After that, I looked at the sky, letting the tears fall down my face. This time, I do not know if I could fix the trouble I caused.

I walked past the Moon Clan's warriors, though none of them stopped me. Anger painted their faces, so I did not stop near them. I went closer to the center of the village, finding a tree that I could climb. I hoisted myself up, getting as far up as I could. I saw the other Clan's warriors walk to the Moon Clan's warriors, inviting them to eat with them. Howling Wolf looked at me in the tree, but I turned away from him. The warriors agreed to eat with them, a sign of a budding friendship. I leaned against the trunk, listening to the gentle roar of their voices and the wind. I held the sheaths in my hands, rubbing my thumbs across the embroidered Wolf and Snow Cat.

Ursus asked Howling Wolf, "Cristata says that Silent Snow told her that she was not the strongest. Who is?"

Howling Wolf answered, "I am. She was my Second."

My chest ached when he said 'was.'

"How was that decided? You have plenty of other warriors that I would think could beat her," the Star Clan's Champion asked them.

"In order to become my Second, she had to fight them all, then fight me. She beat them," Howling Wolf said .

First Son and the Elder shook hands after stepping outside of the building they were in. The Elder came over to where everyone was eating and announced, "We welcome the Moon Clan as allies. We will aid them in their times of need, and we will return the favor when they need us."

First Son looked around. "Where is Snow?"

Howling Wolf gestured to the tree where I was sitting. "Take a guess."

First Son looked over to me then to Howling Wolf. "I am going over there."

"Suit yourself." The angry Enforcer took a drink of water. "Maybe you can talk sense into her."

First Son came over to the base of the tree I was in. "Snow? Can we talk?"

I looked down at him, before helping him up into the tree. I sat back, still rubbing the embroidery.

"Snow? Are you all right?"

I looked at him and asked if he meant physically or something else.

"We will start with physically."

140

I answered with a yawn.

"Then how about emotionally?"

I shook my head, eyeing the warriors enjoying their meal together.

He grabbed the sheaths from my hands. "Howling Wolf made this? He said that he gave it to you after you became his Second."

I told First Son that Howling Wolf used 'was' in his description.

"He is just angry at you."

I told him that I figured that, but I could not see why, beyond poisoning them to keep them safe.

"You poisoned us, so you would be the one killed if it came down to it?" I nodded to him again, grateful that he understood that. "If you did not come, who do you think would have?"

I pointed to Howling Wolf, because First Son was the heir to the Elder, not the Enforcer.

"What would have you done if he poisoned you and ran off to die in a fight without you?"

I looked at him, feeling the pain in my chest. I pointed to my heart and mimed breaking.

"Exactly. We spent the entire time coming here wondering if we were walking into a trap, or if you had already been killed. What do you think he would have done if you were dead?"

I thought about it, before giving him the symbol for war.

He chuckled. "You understand so much, yet so little."

My head tilted to the side as he laughed. "Snow, you cannot see it? You have spent a few years with him, pulling his cold heart from its barrier of ice. If something happened to you, I do not know if we would ever get the warm Wolf back." He looked over to the warriors. "He made you his Second, before he realized what a force you are for him. He is still trying to come to grips with those emotions for a woman who throws herself at the world, not caring if she survived or not."

I asked him how I could do my job as an Enforcer if he hinders me due to his emotions.

"The only thing you need to do is work with him. You two are the Enforcers, so you need to follow his lead, even if that means he will be in danger as well. He has been an Enforcer for a long time and has survived this long. He can take care of himself." He leaned forward, closer to me. "You, on the other hand, need to stop trying to prove to us that you are worthy of your name and Clan. We already know that you are." He sat back, before climbing down. "Just some things to think about. I will grab you some food before we leave, if you do not decide to join us."

I debated whether to follow him but decided against it. I was sure Howling Wolf needed some time away from me, since I caused him so many problems. I waited until the warriors were ready to part ways and jumped down at the last possible second. Howling Wolf grabbed me, keeping me next to him, to make sure I did not run off like he was sure I was going to do. The other warriors gave us space as they escorted me back to the village. We did not talk the entire time back, silence filling the forest around us.

Chapter 13

"You are going to be punished for what you did, Silent Snow," the Elder spoke, his voice edging on angry. "You do not poison your Elder or your Enforcer. What would have happened to the village if we were attacked while we were out?"

I shrank down. I did not think about something like that happening, so it never occurred to me.

He looked over to Howling Wolf and said, "I am putting you in charge of her punishment. I assume that you will make her understand how wrong she was in doing this."

"Yes, Honorable Elder," Howling Wolf replied. He glared at me. "Get up." I did as he said, standing up, following him out the door. He walked us over to where we had trained before the Enforcer test. "Give me your daggers."

I handed the daggers to him but kept the sheaths on.

"Sit." He pushed me down onto the ground. "Stay. If you move, I'll make sure you wish you never caused all of this damage."

I stayed where he pushed me, trying to figure out what his game was. While he planned, I stared into the trees, waiting to see what would happen. Twilight came over me, followed by the night, and Howling Wolf was still not back. I yawned and stretched to keep myself awake.

After some time, he came back, carrying two sparring sticks. "Since you seem to think that you can handle anything, come at me. If you beat me, I will stop your punishment. If not, we will continue it."

He tossed one of the sticks to me. Since I did not know how to use it except as a spear, I was not ready when he attacked. He kept knocking me back, using the stick to push me. I just kept blocking each of his hits, falling into the rhythm of the fight. I do not know how long he had been on the offensive, but my arms were weak, and my body ached from lack of sleep or rest. He slammed me into the ground, and I could not get my body to stand back up.

He took the stick away from me. "Stay."

He walked away, leaving me where I fell. I bit my tongue to stay awake, not wanting to see what would happen if he came back, and I was asleep. Too soon, exhaustion and pain from my muscles overtook me. I slid to the ground, unable to keep my eyes open any longer.

For three days, Howling Wolf would come back to spar with me using the sticks. Every time, he would push me down, and I was told not to move. My stomach grumbled from lack of food; my mouth dry from lack of water. My eyes burned from staying awake.

One of the times that he came for me, I dropped my guard to let him hit me down. I just wanted him to knock me out, so that I could get some rest. He stood over me. "You think that I am going to help you rest? Not happening." He took the sticks and walked away.

On the fourth day, Sparrow came and gave me some water, and a little bit of food, though my stomach rebelled. I tried to keep it down, but I could not. On the fifth day, Sparrow gave me more food and water. First Son saw what Howling Wolf was putting me through. He took my dagger from Howling Wolf's belt, throwing it into the ground. "Since you're not taking care of her, I challenge you to a test of taking."

I was confused, my mind fuzzy from the lack of rest.

"You want her? You can have her. She is weak and will never be good enough," Howling Wolf spat to his friend.

First Son looked at Howling Wolf. "What has gotten into you?"

Sparrow helped me stand, getting me away from the two of them. She took me into the forest, where I heard other voices.

I pointed for her to get into the tree. She climbed it, while I looked in on the Wood Elves who were not a part of the Moon Clan. There were three of them, but another popped up behind me and put a knife to my throat.

"Looks like I found us a prize." He pushed me forward, where the other Wood Elves were. I was so weak from the punishment Howling Wolf was putting me through, I could not see straight enough to fight back.

Another of them said, "Look at that hair! I think the Seller would like this one." He gave me an evil grin.

There was a sharp pain in my temple before darkness clouded my vision.

Chapter 14

I woke up, pain radiating from my head as light danced through the covered cage. I reached for my daggers but remembered that Howling Wolf still had them. I looked around; my arms bound behind me.

"She woke up, finally," one of my captors said. One was driving the cage, the other three were in the back with me. The one who spoke grabbed my chin in his hand, forcing me to look at him. "She has got some pretty green eyes. I wonder if that is normal for City Elves."

"Well, the Seller will know for sure. Maybe he will give us a large bounty for her," another remarked.

"She is easy on the eyes, so I think he should be able to fetch a good price for her."

I stiffened, realizing that they were going to sell me back into slavery.

The covered cage stopped, and I could hear more voices outside. They picked me up, pushing me onto my face outside of the cage. "Do not damage the merchandise." The driver came around and picked me up. He licked his thumb and wiped the dirt from my cheek and said, "We need her to look perfect to get the best price." He led me to a large tent, one I recognized at the edge of my memories. I tried to plant my feet, but they forced me forward.

The tent doors opened, revealing the Seller, a City Elf that I knew, who sold me into slavery the first time. "What is this?" he asked over his half-moon glasses.

"We found her in the forest. Isn't she a beaute?" The driver pushed me closer to the Seller.

The Seller stood up and circled around me. "She looks familiar." He grabbed my hair between his fingers, looking at the bright silver strands. "I knew I recognized her!" He grabbed my wrist and saw the brand. "This is 13-87-22! She escaped her last master after setting the wooden town on fire." He looked gleeful, as he handed gold pieces to my captors. They left me with him. "Oh, 13-87-22... you've grown into a fine woman."

He went to his desk, where he pulled the silver ball with my voice in it. My eyes widened at it, amazed that he still had it. "You want your voice back?" He sat in his chair, pulling me closer to him. "I know that you have been taught how to be a good girl." He caressed my cheek with his hand, but I turned my head and bit him. He slapped me across the face. "Maybe some time relearning what you are would remind you of your place!"

He threw me onto the floor, but I did not fall back completely. He kicked me onto the ground, his foot on my chest. "Do not think you can be above your place, slave."

I hissed at him, but the Snow Cat was locked in her den from exhaustion.

He pressed his foot into my throat. "Keep digging a hole for yourself." After a battle of wills, I looked away first. He took his foot from my neck. "Stay down, unless you want to taste the leather of the whip."

He went back to his work, tallying up and balancing his books. After what felt like forever, he stretched and stood up. He grabbed me off the ground and pressed me into the bars that held the other slaves. The City Elves moved farther away from me, making signs to ward off evil towards me.

"The Cursed One."

"Kinkiller."

"Murderer."

The Seller laughed. "Even they do not want you near them." He pulled me away from the bars, dragging me out of his office. He pushed me toward a covered caravan, but I threw myself at the ground instead. He tried to grab me, but I kept kicking him away. He struck me hard in the stomach with his boot, knocking the wind from me, while causing more pain. "Now, look what you made me do. Get up."

I shook my head, refusing.

"Get up, or I will make you get up."

I shook my head again.

"I heard about the silver-haired slave who rebelled constantly. I guess that bitch was you."

He grabbed me by the hair and yanked me up. He shoved me into a pole, attached the chains to my upper arms, then removed the ropes that bound my wrists. "This is for thinking that you are above your lot in this life."

The whip whistled before it hit my back. I screamed silently in pain, my muscles still aching from the fight, punishment, and now the whip.

He stepped around to my front. "Are you going to keep fighting me?"

I spat at him, giving him my answer.

"You will pay for that. How much pain can you handle, 13-87-22? I know your body is covered in scars from rebelling, so maybe I need to break you before trying to sell you again."

I braced myself as he whipped me. Each time I heard the whistling of the whip flying through it air, I tried to relax my body so it would not hurt as much. I went into the place in my mind, where I could disassociate from the pain, somewhere I felt safe. There, I found myself in the spring near the Moon Clan village, using that image to keep myself from feeling everything he did to me. My body still screamed with each lash, but at least I was able to handle it better.

After what seemed like forever, the Seller stopped. He undid the chains, and I fell to the ground, my body giving out. He dragged me to the covered caravan and threw me inside. I could not fight him as he let me bleed on the ground of his caravan.

"Now, are you going to be a good slave, and do as you are told?" He smiled, telling me what he wanted from me.

I shook my head, more willing to bleed than to deal with what he was planning.

He shoved me out of his caravan, dragged me over to the whipping stake, and chained me back up. "Maybe you will be more agreeable after a night in the forest."

I fell into a pained sleep, trying to use the time alone to regain some semblance of strength. Hours later, I woke up with the dawn, the smell of food in the air.

The Seller cooking something in the pot. He knew better than to let his slaves starve, so they ate his scraps. He caught me looking and brought the delicious smell over to me, in a bowl. "Want some?" he asked.

I looked at him, knowing that it was a trap. Yet, I could not muster up spitting in it to ruin it.   "You just have to do as I say, and I will reward you." He waved the bowl under my nose, letting the smell waft up to me. He went back to the fire, leaving the bowl on the ground in front of me. He watched me. "Beg like the dog you are, and I will let you have some."

I kicked the bowl, knocking it over.

Rage covered his face, as he stood back up. He grabbed the bowl in one hand and the back of my head in the other. He smeared my face in the residue in the bowl, before going back to his fire. The other City Elves stayed silent, not wanting to incur the wrath of the whip.

After he finished eating, he looked at me. "I need to teach you some manners, it seems." He looked to the other City Elves. "Maybe you could be the lesson for them." He pulled them out of the cage, forcing them in front of me. He grabbed the silver ball with my voice and put it in my mouth. It warmed as it became a part of me once again. He punched me in the face, blood clouding my vision. "This is what awaits you if you think that you could be anything other than slaves!"

The whip whistled, and I screamed when it hit. My voice was rough, my vocal cords moving through their lack of use.

"Music to my ears," he said happily. He kept whipping me, listening to my screams, until my throat was sore from it. "This is why yo—" His voice was cut off with the sound of blood. I could not see what was going on, but from the looks of the other City Elves, the Seller was dead.

They whispered, "Wood Elves."

I wanted to get my hopes up, but I was so far away from the Moon Clan's village that it could not have been them. Someone released me from the chains, catching me as I fell. Pain shot through me as the nerves reactivated in my back. I screamed out loud, feeling the body holding me stiffen.

"It is all right, Snow. I have you." Howling Wolf leaned in closer to me, so I could see his face.

Tears ran down my face.

First Son spoke to the City Elves, "The slave trader is dead. You are all free now."

"And where can we go?" the older man from the family asked him. "We are City Elves, slaves for humans. We have nowhere else to go! We have been branded, so if we are caught again, we will be punished like the Cursed One was."

"You can go into the forest and make a new home for yourselves."

"With what skills? We are domestic servants, not Wood Elves. We cannot survive outside the cities." He looked over to me. "And we definitely do not want to be anywhere near her. She is a Kinkiller and a murderer."

Howling Wolf roared, "Do not talk about our Snow like you know her!"

I touched his face. "Please, do not..." My voice was still rough and scratchy, but at least it was back. "They do not understand..."

"I understand well enough, Cursed One. You killed your last master and set the City Elves living with you on fire! You burned them to death, Kinkiller!" he shouted before turning to First Son. "You have caused enough damage here. We can only pray to the Goddess Above that She will protect us."

First Son sighed as he walked back to Wolf and me. "It is hopeless." He whistled lowly when he saw my back. "We will have to walk it, because anything more jostling, and her back will keep bleeding."

Howling Wolf lifted me up. "Let us go home, Snow."

"Get the ledger. Black cover, yellow pages." I winced in pain as I shifted. First Son searched and grabbed the book then tucked it into his top.

The other warriors stared at the City Elves, then turned away. They could not understand why they would choose bondage over freedom. Howling Wolf held me close to him, and I listened to his heart beating in his chest. I wanted to sleep, but every time I tried, he would jolt me. "I am sorry, but you cannot fall asleep until Grandfather tells us that you will wake up again."

I do not know how long we walked, but the lashes in my back scabbed over, the blood deciding to stop flowing from them.

"Wolf! First Son!" Sparrow's voice called from ahead of us. "Is that... Snow?" she asked as Howling Wolf carried me. "There is so much blood... I will get Grandfather ready for her."

Grandfather gasped when he saw me, rushing Howling Wolf to set me on the table. He set me face down, not wanting to put pressure on my back. They tore away the destroyed shirt and Howling Wolf cursed, "That bastard."

"I hope you killed him for this." There was a hardness in Grandfather's voice that I never heard before.

"He is dead," I confirmed then fell into a violent coughing fit. Blood dripped from my mouth, and I wondered if it was because my vocal cords were damaged beyond repair.

"Sh, Silent Snow." Grandfather touched my hair "Just rest now." He turned to Howling Wolf. "Grab Sparrow and let us get started." With that, he put a cup of sleeping poison to my lips, and I drank until there was nothing left. I let the darkness take me into a painless sleep.

Chapter 15

I woke up to someone snoring. I tried to move, but my body was still in pain. I knew that I was naked, but a light sheet was covering me. I looked to see Howling Wolf asleep in the chair next to me. I gave him a low whistle, and he jolted up.

He saw that I was awake, and he lightly touched my face. "We did what we could, but you will have to be careful for a while. The skin is trying to knit itself back together, but because of how deep the lashes were, it will take more time than normal." He got closer to me, and grief filled in his eyes. "I am so sorry, Snow."

"Why?" I asked.

He gave me a small smile. "Because if I did not push you into the brink of exhaustion, you would never have been taken. Sparrow told us what happened. First Son had just challenged me for the Test of Taking, when we saw her take you into the forest. She said that you heard voices and told her to climb a tree to be safe. Then she watched as they overpowered you and knocked you out. They did not stay in the area long, so as soon as it was safe, she ran to tell us that you were gone. We searched for three days for any sign of you."

He grabbed my hand carefully. "Then a scout said there was a slave trader travelling in the area, and we took the chance. We heard you screaming, though we did not know it was you at the time. When we realized that he was whipping someone, First Son put an arrow through him, while I got you down from that contraption he had you chained in. You were covered in so much blood, and we were not sure how much you had lost." He kissed the back of my hand. "Snow, can you ever forgive me for this?"

I whispered, "Yes."

He stood up and kissed my hair. "Get some more sleep, Snow. I will keep watch, so you will be safe."

I nodded and felled back into the dreamless healing sleep.

The next time I woke up, I felt a little better. Howling Wolf stayed by my side the whole time I slept. Sparrow came in a few times to check on me and the wounds. First Son brought food and water for Howling Wolf and I, though I could not eat normally without wanting to throw it back up. A couple days of more rest, and Grandfather told Howling Wolf to take me to the spring to get the blood washed off me.

He carried me to the spring and set me down in the water then slid in himself. He took care of me, helping me to wash the blood and gross off me. In the water, I felt like I could handle myself, so I carefully pulled away from him, letting the water keep me light. Howling Wolf's eyes filled with worry as the water around me tinged red. I turned so he could see my back, the wounds not leaking blood.

After he felt like I was clean enough, he patted my back dry with a cloth, letting me dry my front. Grandfather gave me a very light linen dress to wear while healing. Sparrow told Wolf to take me to her house after we were done, but he took me to his instead. He flopped me on the soft bed, letting me hog the single pillow. He sat in the chair while I slept, and a few times, I caught him asleep in it.

After a few more days, I told him to sleep in the bed, because he looked like his back was sore from trying to sleep in the chair. "You have already seen and slept next to me naked," I reminded him, before getting into a coughing fit.

Grandfather was not worried about me coughing up blood, until he knew that my back would heal fully, just adding to the myriad of scars. Once he deemed me healed enough to be able to walk without help, he checked my vocal cords with his magic. He found that I was right in thinking they were bleeding because they were not used for so long. He believed that as long as I do not overdo it, they will heal, and I could speak normally.

A month after my abduction, I healed enough to go through the basic warmups with Howling Wolf, to help get my muscles stretched out and limber. Grandfather said that they would also help to strengthen my back, so he allowed it.

One day, Howling Wolf and First Son sat me down alone. "What did the City Elves mean by calling you a Kinkiller?"

I looked at the two of them, wondering if it would help them understand me better. "Easier to show than tell." I walked them over to Grandfather's. "Blood fire memory magic," I told the older man.

"All right, what is this about?" he asked more of the males than me.

"She was called a Kinkiller by the City Elves that were with her in the Seller's travelling caravan. They claimed that she burned the other City Elves alive," First Son explained. "She said that it is easier to show rather than tell us."

Grandfather's face softened as he looked at me. "You never told them?"

I shook my head. "Could not."

"Are you sure? Bringing those up like this could make them harder to forget," he asked, compassion in his voice.

"No, but they need to see to understand," I answered.

"Well, grab Sparrow since she has been asking questions about how City Elves would refuse to fight back against their slavery," he told First Son, who ran out the door to do as the older male asked.

He returned with Sparrow, who looked confused. "What is going on? First Son said it was urgent."

"Snow wants to show us something," Howling Wolf explained. "Grandfather said to bring you, so you could see why some would choose slavery over rebelling."

"Is everyone ready?" Grandfather asked before taking us into the room with the large fire. I stayed as far away from it as possible, still not able to get close without an assault of memories. He cut my finger and the blood dripped into the fire.

"Show us why City Elves do not rebel, and why you are called Kinkiller, Silent Snow," the Elder came in and commanded.

I took a deep breath and closed my eyes, trying to ignore the smell of burning blood. I looked to see the smoke rising, revealing my memories to them.

"Bring me 13-87-22," the master told one of his scantily clad female slaves.

They dragged me into the room, as I fought to get away. I knew what was to come, since this master was known for buying and breaking virgins. I was maybe fourteen hundred years old as I struggled against those who carried me. It took four of them, each holding a limb to get me even close to the room.

"Chain her," he told the other slaves as they threw me onto the bed. I tried to get up and away, but they held me down. They chained my wrists and ankles to the bed. I screamed silently, trying to get them to release me. "Leave us," he told his slaves, and with that they escaped into the hall. The master laid next to me. "Such beautiful hair, 13-87-22." He held it to his nose and inhaled its scent.

I looked at him, tears falling from my eyes. In silence, I begged for him to stop touching me.

"Do not worry. You will learn to love what I am going to teach you." He leaned over me, pressing his lips to mine.

I bit him on the lip, drawing blood.

He jerked back, slapped me across the face.

I glared at him through my blurred vision.

He pulled away from me, ripping the snaps on the dress he required his slaves to wear to easier access. I spat at him when he came over me. He hit me again, and the bruise on my cheek darkened.

"Maybe this will make you more amenable." He got up, and I saw him grabbing something and pouring it into a cup. He came back to me and said, "Drink this, 13-87-22." He poured it into my mouth, but I refused to let it get down my throat; the taste of the bitter herb of the sleeping poison stayed on my tongue. He stopped, and I spat the disgusting fluid back at him, my blood mixed in. He hit me a third time, and forced my mouth open with his hands. He poured the drink in and then hit me, so I ended up swallowing some. Not a lot, but it was enough.

I tried to fight off the effects of the sleeping poison, but I was not able to. Everything became a haze before I fell asleep.

I woke up later, my body hurting and sore.

"Take her away," the master commanded his slaves.

When they pulled me up warm blood dripped from between my thighs.

"Next time you fight me, you will taste the whip, 13-87-22," he told me as the males carried me passed him.

The memory skipped to another time the master had me called into his chambers. I came in, almost willingly. My back had been whipped raw, and if I did not answer his summons, it would be worse. Along the way, something cold press against me. I turned to see a Snow Cat spirit drawing me into another room. I followed her into the room, where I gasped. I saw her pelt and those of kittens lying around the room. I touched it before looking to the spirit.

Her cold voice came into my mind. "I can give you the strength you desire to fight back, but I need something in return."

I nodded to her, leaning forward to accept her into me. That's when my eyes became blue for the first time. With the Snow Cat's spirit in me, I walked into my master's bed chamber. My hair covered my face and eyes.

He did not notice the change in me. "Come to me, 13-87-22. Be the good slave I know you can be."

I stepped up to where he sat.

He touched my face, moving my silver hair away from my eyes. "Why are they blue?" he asked as I let the Snow Cat launch my body at him.

I tackled him onto the bed and placed my hands around his throat. He tried to fight me off, but the strength of the Snow Cat was too much for him to escape from. His eyes rolled back into his sockets, falling unconscious.

I stopped before he died, knowing that I would be killed if he passed. The Snow Cat howled for vengeance against him. I pushed her down, telling her that he would die, but not like this. Instead, I went over to where the sleeping poison was and grabbed a cupful of it. I poured the drink down his throat, his body swallowing it without his knowledge. I laid his face down in the pillow, letting him suffocate himself. The Snow Cat was angry at her denial of killing him herself, but she accepted my decision. I left the master there to die, going back to my quarters, where the other slaves stayed away from me, hoping they would not get punished next.

The memory changed to show a myriad of other ones, each one showing the scars that I gained from rebelling, including those I got from saving other slaves. These slaves did not know what I had done for them, so they all learned to stay away from me. Fear of pain was a strong motivator to stay compliant to the humans. To me, it became a lover, a dancer who I embraced in exchange for thoughts of freedom and taking small pleasures of disobeying the masters I served.

I let the memories show the masters I killed over the centuries. A female master who drowned in her bath after she killed a small child who had spilled red wine during the dinner.

A male who was stomped by his horse, after torturing a stable lad. Another male who died on the hunt when he took me out as bait. A female who died during childbirth when the midwives were worrying about the baby. She died of blood loss when I stitched her up incorrectly. I relived their deaths, and I let the memories show them how I became the Cursed One, since masters seemed to die around me in various accidents.

Then came the final one. The master had heard from his lying guards that there was talk of a rebellion. The master dragged me up to the tallest tower, since he was told that I was the leader of it.

He bent me over the window, forcing me to watch as he set the wooden buildings where the City Elves lived on fire. The heat and the smell of burning flesh was strong as it hit me. He raped me from behind, forcing me to watch the flames and listen to the screams below. When he finished, he grabbed my hair and pulled my back to his chest. I dropped to my knee, rolling my shoulder down, and threw him out the window, using the same move Howling Wolf wondered where I learned. I watched and heard him crash into one of the burning buildings below.

I threw on the torn clothes and raced down to the burning village below. I dodged around guards, hiding when I heard them stomping closer by letting the Snow Cat take over. We made it out the front doors, throwing something heavy in front of them, trapping the humans inside the stone building. I ran to where I heard the screams. The humans had blocked the City Elves in the wooden houses, so I had to fight to get them open. I kicked the doors open, getting those I could out. Even though I was the Cursed One, they all knew that I was there to save them. I ran through the village, ignoring the searing heat of the inferno, trying to find more survivors. I found some, but not everyone was alive when I reached them.

By the time the guards were able to get the front doors open, I stood outside the gates with the surviving City Elves. They thanked me for saving them, most apologized for calling me the Cursed One and other names. We heard the humans coming, but they made a wall between them and I. The oldest, the Patriarch of the City Elves in this house, yelled for me to run. I did as he said and took off, letting the Snow Cat guide my steps. I kept the memory going until I reached Howling Wolf, wanting his Wolf pelt to get warm again.

The memories faded from the smoke, as the fire did down. Sparrow cried into First Son's shoulder, "Goddess Above..."

"They called me Kinkiller because I doubt any of those City Elves survived the guards. Especially after the body of that sadistic bastard was found," I said, my voice too quiet as I looked to Sparrow. "Fear is one of the strongest ways of controlling someone. If you are taught to fear the humans for the viciousness they possess, and seeing it firsthand, most are unwilling to fight against them."

"I am sorry that you had to see this, but I would not have been able to explain it as it needed to be." I looked over to Howling Wolf. "This is why I throw my life into everything I have. What you have tried to build in the past few years has to battle against the centuries of hoping that the humans would finally kill me in their rage for my rebellion."

"Can you give us space, Silent Snow?" the Elder asked, putting his hand on my shoulder in an almost fatherly gesture.

"Of course." I left them in the large building. I could have gone to where the other Clans members were, but I needed time alone to push those memories back to where they belonged. So, I went into the tree the Clan had designated as mine and used it to climb onto Sparrow's house. I remembered the look in Howling Wolf's eyes and knew something had changed again.

They thought they knew what I had been through, but to see it firsthand was a different story.

I put my hands behind my head as padding and laid back. I closed my eyes to the bright sky, using a mental image of the Snow Cat to push the memories back into their respective places, before putting bars over them to keep them contained.

"Snow?"

I opened my eyes to see Howling Wolf in my tree.

"Are you okay? Grandfather is worried that by showing us your memories that you would not be able to contain them anymore."

"I will be all right. What about you? Sparrow was crying, then First Son and you looked like you were going to start," I asked him. "You saw the darkest parts of my life, so I understand if you cannot see me the same as bef—"

He leaned forward and put a finger to my lips. "Stop with this, Snow. I have seen you kill before; the dead look in your eyes after you killed those slavers. I now know why you slaughtered them. You are my Second and seeing those kinds of memories will not change that."

"'Was' your Second. You said that I 'was' your Second." I pointed out as I sat up.

"I was angry because I had been so worried that we would only find you dead from the Star Clan's challenge. It could have been a trap, so the fact that you went, and we did not know if you were still there... Then we found out that not only did you win, but you were also eating with them, after brokering an alliance. Seeing you fine just made me realize that you could take care of yourself." He sighed. "My anger and worry took over me."

"Why would it bother you so much that I could take care of myself? It is the reason why you trained and tested me. I have to be able to do my job with you, without having to worry whether or not you are going to stop me every time there's a fight."

"It bothers me because I want to—" he changed mid-sentence, "—I need to protect you. More than just as I would another Clans member."

I tilted my head. "Why?"

"Is it not obvious?" He laughed. "I guess not. You see a lot, but you miss other things." He coughed to buy time before speaking again. "As for you doing your job, you do it with me. You do not go running off to take on the world without me. That is your place as my Second. But the first hint of a battle, I want

171

you at my side." He pulled my daggers and sheath from under his shirt. "In order to do that, you need these."

I looked at them and smiled. "Thank you."

"We sharpened them."

I looked at the sheaths. "These are not the same ones. Why are they different?"

"Sparrow made this one, because we could not get the blood cleaned from the other ones."

"Does not matter." I handed it back to him. "These are lovely, but I liked the other ones better."

"They are at my house."

"Then we better go get your sheathes, so these daggers gave a home." I stood up, and we climbed off the roof and back to the ground. We went into his house, where he grabbed the sheath pair I liked. I put them on, feeling better with those familiar weights at my hips.

Chapter 16

"So, has any of the males caught your eye?" Xerinae and her gossip girls grinned at me, while I helped them cook for the Summer Equinox festival by cutting the vegetables.

"She has been so busy sparring with the warriors to keep their skills sharp, that I doubt she has been looking," Sparrow told them.

"Why would they? They are my fellow warriors, so why would any of them try to catch my eyes?" I asked them.

All activity around me stopped, before Xerinae laughed. "You are joking, right? She has to be joking."

Sparrow looked at me, then to the gossip girls, "I do not think she is."

"What are you ladies talking about—Ouch!" The knife slipped and cut my finger. I put it to my mouth to get the pain to stop.

"Do not distract her." Sparrow growled as she grabbed my hand and wrapped my finger.

"Have you told her what this festival is about? For the last couple of years, she was busy with Howling Wolf, so she did not do any of the celebrations or festivals," Xerinae asked Sparrow.

"There was no point in telling her. As you can see, she is hopeless," Sparrow told them, then she turned back to me. "Be careful. How is it you can practically decapitate a sparring dummy, but you cut yourself trying to cut vegetables?"

"Only because you ladies keep pulling my attention away from them," I grumbled when I finished cutting their vegetables. "How did I get wrangled into this in the first place?"

"Simple. We asked for help, and since you are second to none when it comes to knives, it made perfect sense." Xerinae smiled. "And because we need to help get you ready."

I grimaced. "I do not need to get ready. Whenever you ladies say that, I always end up looking weird."

"That is because we are trying to help some of the males see you as the woman you are." Her smiled never faltered; in fact, it grew. "Maybe if one of the males catches your eye, then you can see what many of us have already enjoyed."

"The only thing I want to enjoy is a dip in the spring away from these cooking fires," I mumbled. "Can I leave now?"

"If you do, then we are going to start getting you ready."

"Goddess Above..." I growled.

Xerinae and Sparrow grabbed my upper arms. "You ladies have this?"

"Of course. Get our Snow ready." The gossip girls grinned, and I wondered if that is what prey sees just before they are hunted.

They took me to Sparrow's house.

When I saw Howling Wolf along the way, I mouthed for help.

Sparrow looked at him and said, "You come and try to grab her, and you will be black and blue."

Howling Wolf mouthed an apology to me, and the coward raced to wherever the males go before these things.

Sparrow and Xerinae took off my standard black linens of the Enforcer and undid the bun I wore. Sparrow grabbed my almost hip length braided hair. "It is getting really long."

"Then cut it," I told her. "I could care less about the length, as long as I can pull it back for work."

They just looked at me. "I think I have an idea." Sparrow grabbed a knife and cut through the braid at the base of my neck, cutting my hair to shoulder length. My head felt light, having short hair for the first time in forever.

Xerinae looked at me, a smile on her face. "It suits you better." She then threw me a sleeveless white linen dress with a variety of blue shaded threads embroidered at the hems into a design of snowflakes in the different blue threads.

"Take off the binding wrap."

I growled but took off the binding wrap and put the white dress on.

She adjusted it, the cinched waist going from just under my breasts to my hips, where the dress flared out some going down from my hips to my knees. "You fill it out better than I thought you would. Your breasts are bigger than what I was hoping for." She handed me a piece of blue fabric and said, "Tie this to one side at your waist."

"That's why I have to bind them tightly," I mumbled.

She sat me on the bed, while Sparrow got ready herself in a bright green dress. Xerinae applied simple makeup to my face. She sat back on her heels. "You will definitely be catching eyes tonight."

"I do not want to catch eyes," I grumbled to myself, since both were chattering as they continued getting ready.

Xerinae bid us goodbye, before she left.

I heard First Son's knock on the door, and I ran to it. I opened it to see him standing there, his eyes widened in shock when he saw me. He wore a fancy dark green shirt and pants, his hair styled different than normal. "Please, tell me that this thing is cancelled or that there is a battle or a challenge or anything to get me out of this!"

He laughed, his face lighting up. "No such luck. I am here to act as an escort to Sparrow. Raven will grab Xerinae from her house. Since you are eligible, you do not have an escort."

"Lovely," I growled, as Sparrow came to the door.

First Son's face lit up, seeing Sparrow's beauty. She looked like a Goddess of the forest, the green dress against her dark tan skin. He tried to speak, but he kept stumbling over his words.

"I see that I have rendered you speechless." She looked to me. "You will dance with whoever asks you to dance. You will not run away to the spring or into your tree. If I catch you hiding, you will not get any pillows for a month."

My jaw dropped. "But I like the pillows..."

"Then you will dance with those who are trying to catch your eye. You do not have to stay with them, but you will give them the courtesy of one dance." She put her hands on my shoulders. "Just enjoy yourself. Let us go."

He held his arm out to her, and she grabbed onto it. He gave me one last look. "You have about five minutes before the dances start, so I suggest if you want your pillows, I would be there before they start."

I watched as they walked toward the dance area and waited for a minute, debating if the pillows were worth the warriors seeing me look like this. Deciding that one night was not worth losing the pillows for a month, I grabbed my daggers and sheaths, putting them under the blue ribbon of fabric over my hips. I walked over to the dance area. I snuck around the building, hoping that no one would see me.

"Silent Snow!"

I jumped as Xerinae laughed, Raven on her arm.

"Hiding is not going to help you, Snow."

Behind her, the eligible women chatted with one another. I had never been more grateful for their presence than now. I hid among them, them letting me disappear. Listening to them, I learned that all eligible males are required to dance with all eligible females. After that, those who wanted to pair up did. Those who did not have a partner by the end could pair up with random eligible, male or female, until the end of the dance. Then at the end of the night, if both people wanted to, they would go home together.

On the other side of the dance area, the eligible males came in. I counted them and let out a growl because they outnumbered us, meaning I would have to be out here for longer than I wanted. The women stopped, silent, as they looked at the males. They looked like hungry wolves as they decided who they would dance with first. Howling Wolf's face lit up when he looked at the eligible women.

Ursus and Cristata walked into the area, and I ran over to them, choosing a safer bet. I figured that since the males outnumbered the women, I would not care about who came to ask me for a dance.

"What are you two doing here?" I asked them.

Cristata grabbed my upped arms me and hugged me tightly. "You can talk!"

"Yes, it happened a little after I kicked your partner's butt." I grinned at Ursus, and he returned with a smirk that suggested a rematch. I pulled away from Cristata. "What are you two doing here?"

"We are here because we received a message that our emissary was invited. Since the First Son is yours, I volunteered to be ours. It is a good way for our Clans to have fun together." She smiled broadly.

"How did you convince your Elder to become the Emissary?"

"She did not." Ursus growled, glaring at me. "She took a page from your book and just left. I happened to be patrolling that area when I spotted her. Since she kicks hard, I agreed to be her protector for this, in case we met any enemies along the way. You are a terrible influence."

"Snow! You better not be trying to get out of this!" I winced when Sparrow yelled at me as she came over to us with First Son. She looked at the other Clan's Wood Elves. "You came from the Star Clan?" She gave the two of them an appraising look.

"Sparrow, this is their Champion Ursus, and Emissary Cristata. This is Sparrow, sister to Howling Wolf and partner to First Son," I introduced them.

"Speaking of Howling Wolf..." First Son looked over his shoulder. "Looks like they are about to start, and he has already been snatched up. Looks like you get to start with someone else."

"Wait, what?" Sparrow grabbed me and pulled me to where the other eligible women were standing.

I waited, hoping that they would forget I was there.

"May I have this dance?" One of the warriors stepped up to me.

"I am sorry, but I—" I remembered Sparrow's threat. "I do not know how to dance, and I am not graceful."

His smile never faltered. "That is fine; you will pick it up. And if worse comes to worse, you are light enough that if you step on my toes, it should not hurt too much."

I let him lead me out to where the dancers started. I kept stumbling, as we moved. He pulled me along, until the song ended. When the music changed to a new dance, he asked if I would stay with him.

I shook my head. "I am sorry. I think that one of the other women is trying to catch your eye." I fled from him, trying to calm down. I understood what Xerinae meant, and I wanted to punch her for it. Another warrior came up, and I ended up dancing with most of them, each time, turning them down when they asked me to stay with them. I kept hoping that they would stop asking me.

"Not having fun?" Howling Wolf's voice came up from behind me.

I jumped. "I am!" I tried to get my heart rate to calm down, but it refused.

Another warrior asked me to dance, and I just sighed.

"Sorry, Lynx, this dance is mine." Howling Wolf put his hand on my shoulder.

Lynx apologized and left us alone.

"Why do they keep trying to get me to stay with them?" I asked more of myself, but he heard me.

"Maybe because you impress them? Maybe because they are hoping that they would be the one to take you home tonight." He turned me toward him and led me to the dance. We followed the steps of the dance half-heartedly.

"But why? There are plenty of eligible women who would love to be taken home by the warriors."

"You are an eligible woman," he pointed out.

"I may be eligible, but I am not looking." I gave him a sly look. "What about you? Plenty of the eligible women want you to take them home. I mean, how many dances have we been through. They keep talking about you. Something about your handsome face, something about your voice, your rippling muscles, your tight butt."

He choked. "I do not think that any of them are right for me."

"Well, none of the warriors who keep trying to dance with me are right for me," I admitted. "I mean, I am not pretty; I am not tall like the Wood Elf women. The only thing I have going for me is the fact that I can fight."

He reached over and touched the ends of my shortened hair. "Just because you do not see it does not mean that others don't."

"What are you talking about?"

"Well, for starters, your hair suits you better than when it was long." He touched my cheek. "Whatever face makeup you are wearing brings out your eyes more." He touched the shoulder of the dress. "The dress you are wearing fits your form well. I would say that many of the warriors who are trying to get you to go home with them think you have some sort of beauty."

The song stopped, and we each took a step back from each other.

I grimaced. "I do not want to be asked by any more potential suitors."

He put his hand out. "Then keep dancing with me. I mean, at least then we do not have to keep dealing with new partners. Add in that we do not mind talking to each other, it will make the time pass by faster."

I put my hand in his. "Just to make time go faster."

He put his hands on my hips and jerked back slightly "Are you wearing your daggers?"

"Of course. I do not go anywhere without them. I know you have a knife in your boot, so you cannot say anything." I laughed.

"Carrying weapons to a festival..." He laughed with me. "We are quite a pair, you and I."

We both stopped laughing after a little bit.

"So, how long does this thing last?" I asked him.

"Well, I am guessing that we are getting close to the end, so not much longer. I am surprised you have not tried to escape to the spring yet."

"Sparrow threatened to take away my pillows if I hid," I grumbled. "Speaking of running away, I am surprised that you wanted to stop dancing with the eligible women. I saw your face light up when you saw the pack of them."

"Pack of them would be a good descriptor," He mumbled back. "But I promise you that I did not smile because of the pack of eligible women." He pulled me in closer. "I smiled because I saw you."

I stopped moving and just stared at him. "Why?"

"Well, because…" He looked uncomfortable now, running his fingers through his hair. "Do you think we can escape now?" He grabbed my hand and pulled me toward the spring. He ignored Sparrow calling to us, but I just gave her a wave to put her at ease.

"What is this about, Howling Wolf?" I asked him when we stopped moving.

He took a deep breath, turning to face me. "Snow, I have been trying to figure out how to say this for a while now. I thought that you knew, but Sparrow warned me that you were clueless." He grabbed my hands in his. "I smiled when I saw you because I thought you looked beautiful tonight. I smiled because I was hoping that you would choose me as a partner. I smiled because I love you and have been wanting to tell you for a while now."

I did not say anything for a second, trying to process what he was telling me. "You have felt this way since before the Enforcer test, have you not?" I realized why he was so angry with me because of the challenge.

"Yes."

"Good, because I think I fell in love with you when I saw the sheaths you gave me. I mean, I guess I see how it should have been obvious. Now, I see why the women were giving me a hard time."

He touched my cheek with his hand and leaned in close to me. His lips brushed against mine, an invitation.

I moved closer, pressing my lips to his to accept it. When he pulled away, I finally saw what the other women had been talking about. "This changes things, you know," I told him.

"How so?"

I grinned. "Your sister told me that I was not allowed to take your heart. I am pretty sure that she warned off every other woman that tried to get closer to you, so who knows what she will do when she finds out about this."

He cringed. "Well, if needed, you can stay with me."

"You only have one pillow."

"Hm... You're right. But if we leave now, then we might be able to get your pillow before she gets back to her house." We ran back to Sparrow's house to liberate my pillow, before going to Howling Wolf's home.

I took off the daggers, keeping them close, as he removed his boots with his own knife in it. We crashed on the bed, facing each other. "Howling Wolf?"

"Yes?"

"City Elves do not have partners normally, because the humans can use them to punish someone. So, we do not really have courtships or anything like that. I do not know how to act now."

He reached over, pulling me closer. "Just act the same way you always have been. That is the woman I fell in love with, so I do not want you to change."

I yawned. "I think I can do that."

"Get some sleep, Snow. We can talk more tomorrow."

"Or the day after that... I mean, I thought Wood Elves try to partner for life? At least that is what the stories said."

He kissed my forehead. "Only if you want to."

Chapter 17

"We got a message from the Star Clan," the Elder told Howling Wolf, First Son, and I.

"What is happening?" Howling Wolf asked him.

"They received word about humans in a nearby village, so they want to borrow some of our warriors to assist them." The Elder looked to me. "The humans have ties to the slave trade, so I know that there is no point in trying to stop you."

"When do they need us?" I asked calmly, though inside, I could feel like I was already on edge to fight.

"You leave after this meeting," the Elder answered me. Then to First Son, he said, "I want you there as well, since they call you our Emissary. Raven will keep the village safe while you are all gone. If we get any word that we need to call you back, we will send Lynx since he is the fastest scout." He stood up, "I do not have to tell you how dangerous this will be, so be careful."

"Yes, Honorable Elder," we all replied at the same time.

He waved us off in dismissal. We went outside, and First Son went to get his weapons.

I went with Howling Wolf to his house to get my spear and his bow. "Are you going to be all right?" he asked me as we both put on our black clothes.

"I do not know. I will let you two know if it starts getting to me," I promised, as I checked the daggers in their sheaths and grabbed the whetstone First Son gifted me after Howling Wolf and I started living together. We left his house and waited for First Son.

Sparrow came up to us, handing me a bag. "These are some herbs for your wounds, and some bandages." She hugged her brother, then me. "Stay safe, and make sure you both come home."

"We will." I smiled. "Would not want to worry you for longer than we have to."

"I swear on the Goddess Above, Snow. If you charge into battle without Wolf, I will beat you black and blue," she threatened.

"Howling Wolf has already explained that I will be by his side, not running ahead." I gave her the most innocent smile I could.

"Why do I not believe you?" she grumbled, as First Son came over to us.

"Do not believe what?" he asked her.

"That Snow will not be the first one to fight." She gave First Son a kiss on the cheek. "You better stay safe as well."

"Of course, I will. And I will make sure these two do not get too much blood on them." He pulled her into a kiss on the lips, stealing whatever she was planning on saying.

"All right love birds; we have to go." Howling Wolf grabbed the back of First Son's shirt and pulled him away from his sister. "We will be fine, Sparrow," he promised, as we headed out of the village and into the forest. "Are you going to do your forest walking, Snow?"

I nodded, blinking, bringing out the Snow Cat. Her vision lit up the shadows so I could see the best way forward. Over the past few years that we have been allies with the Star Clan, there was a path between our villages. It was not fully there yet, but I could pick it out with the Snow Cat's vision. The males followed me through the forest, until we reached the message stone. I blinked again; the Snow Cat's vision faded back to my regular sight.

Ursus waved us over to him when we found him. "Thank you for coming, you three."

"You are welcome. It is only the three of us, though, so I hope that is enough," First Son said.

"With the four of us, we should be fine." Ursus looked to me. "We wanted you involved because of the slave trade. We are hoping that we only need you three along with me to defeat them. We are just looking to liberate the slaves, but if there is blood-shedding to be had..." He shrugged.

"City Elves do not like being liberated," I told him. "Last time they killed a slave trader, the City Elves were not exactly happy with it."

"We got a report that the City Elves who are in this grouping were a part of a failed rebellion years ago," he explained.

My eyes widened. "Did they say where from?"

Ursus shook his head. "No, we did not get any of that information. We are hoping that these City Elves are willing to become our liaisons to other liberated ones."

"Here is hoping." I prayed to the Goddess Above that I knew these City Elves, and they would trust me.

"Let us get going." Ursus led the way through the forest.

We left the Star Clan's land, entering Tree Clan's territory, where the human village was hidden. We stayed silent when we reached a cliff above the village. Since this was Ursus's show, we followed his lead.

He looked at me and said, "Get closer, if you can. Do not be seen in your trees. We need an accurate count."

I nodded before sliding down the cliff, using the trees to slow my descent. I climbed up a tall tree that gave me a good vantage point and counted the number of humans I saw roaming the village. There were only males, which was weird, since most villages were a mix of genders. I saw a couple City Elves and understood why. These were not just slavers; they were buyers.

I counted the humans, trying to ignore the bad feeling I was getting. I counted fifty-seven humans with thirty-three City Elves. I took the trees back to where my males were, silent as the falling snow. "There are a lot of them. Fifty-seven males, no females, thirty-three City Elves. I do not think the City Elves will fight, but I also do not know what their captors have done to them."

Someone screamed from below, and my eyes flashed blue.

Howling Wolf grabbed my arm as a warning.

I nodded to him, deferring to him as his Second.

"Did you see a way into the village where we would not be spotted."

"Yes." I reigned in my fury to head off to the village and leaving my males behind.

"Lead the way."

Another scream reached up to us, and I had to fight the urge to run down there without them. Only my loyalty to Howling Wolf stopped me. We walked down the cliff, toward the village. I kept them close to the trees, as a third scream came from the village. I took a deep breath and let it out slowly. I pointed to a blind spot between two buildings, where they would not see us. I then pointed to where I knew the City Elves were being held from prior experience from my slavery.

Ursus pointed Howling Wolf to the top of one of the buildings, since he had a ranged weapon. He pointed me to the second building since I could jump down easier than the males could. Ursus and First Son stayed where they were, ducking behind wooden crates, before going into the back rooms of the two buildings.

We kept watching, and a female City Elf was being dragged to a familiar sight. She screamed and pleaded that she was sorry and that she did not mean to spill the soup.

Howling Wolf stiffened on the rooftop next to me.

Someone thunked the wood under me, followed by a second and a third. I gave one back as an affirmative. I looked to Howling Wolf, and he nodded.

He got an arrow ready as I gave the count.

One, I tapped my foot once. Two, I tapped again. Three, I tapped a third time, then launched myself off the roof. I landed in the center square.

"Let her go!" I yelled out to the human dragging the woman.

"Where did you come from?" He dropped the woman. "Men, we have a visitor!"

Human males poured from around the village to where I was. I counted them, only forty came out, meaning the rest were somewhere not near me.

A single Wood Elf male spoke from the entrance of the largest building. "She is another City Elf. But she wears the clothes of the Moon Clan."

"You are a long way from the Moon Clan, City Elf." Their leader stepped out from the largest building. "But if you want us to take care of you, you just have to say so. We will take good care of you." I wanted to wipe that smile off his lips.

The woman looked at me, recognition crossing her face, "Kinkiller…" she whispered as she made a sign to the Goddess.

The human that was closest to her kicked her down. "What did you say, bitch?"

"She is the Kinkiller! Cursed One! Murderer!" she screeched; fear laced through her voice. She was more scared of me than of them.

"Kinkiller, eh?" The leader looked at me. "That tiny bitch?"

"Maybe you should ask her why I am called that," I spoke, pulling my daggers from their sheaths. "She will tell you how many humans I've killed and how many City Elves died."

"City Elves are weak and useless without their masters. Killing many of them is not an accomplishment," the leader said to me.

"If you truly believe that, then you will not mind dying to prove it."

"I would be careful, humans," the Wood Elf warned. "She wears the clothes of the Moon Clan's Enforcer. I would not underestimate her."

I got into my normal defensive stance, as the familiar thrum of the bow string letting loose an arrow came from Howling Wolf's bow. The leader stumbled as the arrow hit his chest. The humans watched their leader die, before looking back to me. "You see, I came with the Moon and Star Clans. Our combined strength will easily destroy this village."

Male screams came from inside the two buildings where First Son and Ursus were.

"Or, if you think you can kill me, then come and get me."

The humans drew their weapons before the area erupted into chaos.

The doors to the buildings opened, Ursus and First Son joining the fray. Howling Wolf shot arrows at the mass of humans. I saw it all, letting the Snow Cat take over. I looked at the City Elf female. "Stay down and get back, or you might get hurt." She nodded before she scrambled closer to the whipping pole.

The humans came at me, their weapons raised. I used the Snow Cat's speed to attack, letting my rage from the hurt woman and captured City Elves to guide me. I slashed through enemies, as I cut through flesh. I made sure to give them killing blows, not wanting them to get back up. My back hit someone, and I looked to see First Son with his twin axes. We nodded to each other, then switched sides, to take on different opponents. Ursus's large two-handed axe cut through bone as he slashed them. Howling Wolf jumped off the roof of the building and used my spear to join the fight.

It may have taken about ten minutes to thin them down from forty to three. "Where are the rest of your warriors?" First Son asked one of the humans. I looked around and the Wood Elf who had been on the slaver's side was gone.

Someone screamed, and the smell of smoke wafted from where the City Elves were being held, followed by a malicious smile on the human's face. "The City Elves!"

Howling Wolf and I ran to the two-story building where City Elves were kept.

I slashed through the last of the humans, Howling Wolf killing them alongside me. Although I tried to get the door open, I was not strong enough. "Ursus!" I yelled, hoping his axe could get through the wood. I ran around the building, trying to find a way into the building. Howling Wolf and I found a window high up. "Give me a lift," I told him. He looked unsure, until I shouted, "Hurry! I will try to get them out, if I cannot then I will come back out through this window." He readied himself, as I stepped into his hands, and he pushed me up. I caught the window ledge, smashed it in, and climbed inside.

The smell and smoke were thick, so I used my black linen shirt to cover my nose and mouth. I called out, "Is there anyone here?!" I ran through the building, finding a couple City Elves on the second floor. I found another window and used the butts of my daggers to smash them outward. "Get out!"

I saw the stairs and hopped over the railing. "Is there anyone still alive down here?!" Memories mixed with reality, as I needed to save them, since I could not save everyone last time. There was a faint yell from below. I ran through the building, finding the way into the cellar through the pantry. I found the rest of the City Elves there, pressing themselves as low as they could to the floor.

"Snow! Where are you?" Ursus shouted as he busted through the door.

"In the back, in the cellar!" I yelled back, hoping he could hear me above the crackling flames. "Come on! We need to get out of here!" I helped them stand, the smoke hurting our lungs. I got them up the stairs into the main room, where Ursus got them outside. I got the last City Elf out of the building, the pantry collapsing above me. I tumbled into the cellar, trying to keep the flames away from my face. I tried to get back up the stairs, but the debris blocked it. I searched the cellar, trying to find a way out.

"Snow!" I barely heard his voice above the loud crackling flames. I knocked on the floor, hoping he would hear or feel it.

"Goddess Above, please do not let this be where I die," I prayed, hoping She could hear me above the loud sounds of the fire. The floor gave way above me, Ursus's axe trying to get through the floor. I used my daggers to try to tear at the wood from my side. My shirt was failing to keep the smoke from my lungs. The heat of the fire was becoming too much, and I fell to the ground. The Snow Cat hissed at the fire, since it was something we could not fight. She returned to her den; her extra strength could not help me.

Ursus's axe made it through the floor, "She is down here!" he yelled. They tore open the floor, making a big enough hole for Howling Wolf. He jumped down into the cellar, picked me up, and handed me to Ursus and First Son. He jumped out of the hole, Ursus helping him out of it. First Son carried me out of the burning building. He set me on the ground. Howling Wolf and Ursus came out of the building next.

"Are you well, Snow?" Howling Wolf asked.

"Minor injuries." I gave him a thumbs up. "Goddess Above, I hate fire."

First Son walked over to talk with the City Elves, "Are all of you doing all right?"

I sat up to their murmurs and whispers calling me a Kinkiller, Cursed One, and Murderer.

The woman that we saved first chastised them. "Stop it. You think she would have risked her life to save us if she was a Kinkiller?" She stepped up to First Son. "We will be fine, just a little bit of smoke inhalation and minor burns."

"Thank the Goddess Above." Sickening relief washed over me. I looked at Howling Wolf, tears filling my eyes. "We saved them all."

"You saved them, Snow." His eyes were soft, "I know that it does not make up for those you could not save, but you saved all of them." He grabbed my hand and pulled me up. "She is not a Kinkiller. The master she was forced to serve killed the City Elves when he burned their buildings to the ground. She tried to save them like she did now, but she could not get to them all."

"What are you planning to do?" First Son asked them, hoping they would not bite his head off like the last City Elves they liberated.

"We are City Elves, and we have heard stories about Wood Elves, along with this experience." The woman became their de facto leader. She swept her long, light brown hair back over her shoulders. She stood tall, her blue eyes glittering with worry. "I do not know what we are going to do now."

"If you need a safe place, our Clan can take you all in," Ursus offered. "It is not like the cities, but if this City Elf can learn how to live in the forest with us, maybe you all can, too." He then also added, "But if you prefer something else, I am sure we can figure out an arrangement. Maybe a village for City Elves where they can be protected by both of our Clans."

The woman looked to the other City Elves. "We do not want to stay slaves."

"Wood Elves do not have slaves," the males all said at once.

The woman looked to me. "Is that true?"

I nodded. "I came to the Moon Clan after running from my former master. They accepted me as one of their own. I will never allow anyone to own my life again." I smiled. "I like my freedom too much."

"Freedom..." She sounded wistful. She shook her head and looked to Ursus. "We will go with you and make plans on whether we will stay with the Wood Elves or make our own establishment."

"Sounds good to me," Ursus replied. "We will leave whenever your people are ready. It is less than a day's trek—"

"It will take a day and a half," I interrupted him. "City Elves are shorter than Wood Elves. Since they are not used to walking long distances or in the woods, it will take longer to get there."

Ursus looked to the City Elves then back to me. "So, you are not just abnormally small?"

I growled. "No. Keep teasing me, and you will kiss the dirt."

He made a face to the City Elf woman. "Do all City Elves have large bravado?"

She laughed. "Would not know. We have to keep our true personalities secret, lest the humans decide that we are no longer useful to them."

"What happens if you are no longer useful?"

"If we are lucky? We are sold. If we are unlucky..." I told him, my voice trailing off. "That is why my former bastard of a master decided to torch the buildings where the City Elves lived."

"City Elves are property. So, if someone loses them to, let us say a fire, the kingdom will compensate that master for the loss," the City Elf woman explained.

"Then why would you not fight back? I mean, you already have the worry that you will be killed if you are no longer useful, on the whim of a human," Ursus asked her.

She hesitated. "I have only been whipped once in my life. It was the worst pain I have ever felt, including bones breaking and childbirth. The fact that your City Elf is covered in lash scars is a testament to her willingness to take the pain. If I never have to feel the whip in my back again, then it would do anything to stop it."

"Ursus, you have never had to feel what it is like. She is right in that it is the worst pain you can imagine." I hoped he would understand.

He looked contemplative, then grabbed the whip from the ground. "Whip me."

"What?" the City Elf woman and I asked him at the same time.

"I need to understand what you two are talking about, to understand why City Elves would choose bondage. If we are to help them, then I need to know how I can connect with them."

"You do not have to—"

I cut her off. "Are you sure? Are you absolutely positive that you need to feel this to understand their plight?"

"Yes." He did not hesitate.

I looked at the City Elf woman. "Get your people away from here; I do not want them to see this." She nodded and gathered them up. "We will meet you in the large stone building over there." I then pointed to the building standing alone at the edge of the village. The other City Elves followed her. I looked to First Son and Howling Wolf. "I am not going to ask you two to help me. Maybe you should go with the City El—"

"Not a chance," Howling Wolf interrupted me. "Tell me what to do."

"Ursus, pass your axe to First Son." I waited for him to comply. "Strip off your top."

He took it off and threw it at the ground.

"Knock the wind out of him." My voice was cold.

First Son punched Ursus in the stomach, Ursus's breathing to become ragged. "Grab him and bring him with me." The two Moon Clan Elves lunged forward and grabbed onto Ursus hard enough he could not fight. They carried him to where the whipping pole was. By the time he was chained to it, he was finally able to breathe again. "Last chance, slave. Comply with your master or feel the taste of the leather." My voice was even, despite the anger and rage I felt for myself for doing this to a friend.

"I will never comply, human," he growled at me, as I stood behind him.

I readied the whip, but Howling Wolf took it from me. I gave him three fingers for three lashings, a regular occurrence for most City Elf punishments. I pointed between Ursus's shoulder blades. Howling Wolf's eyes widened, but he nodded.

"I am sorry, Ursus," I whispered

"Just—"

The whip whistled through the air; it slammed into the spot between his shoulder blades. He screamed in pain, grabbing onto the chains that held him. The next lash went a bit to the left, then the third to the right. His skin was covered in sweat and blood, dripping down his back. He was having problems pushing through the pain to breathe. I did not warn him about the secondary burns from the sweat getting into the wounds.

"Leave him there." I pulled the two Moon Clan Elves away from the area. "Take his axe and shirt and go to where the City

Elves are. Send the City Elf Matriarch back here. She will know what to bring."

They looked like they were going to argue, but I shook my head in a warning. They did as I said, leaving Ursus and I. I sat on the ground, watching the blood start to clot, but every time sweat encountered the wounds, his breathing was pained. The City Elf woman came over to where I was.

She sucked in a breath as she saw Ursus's back. "You really did it."

"He is a stubborn ox, so he would have found a way to do this. At least me doing it means it would not get out of hand. Did you bring the kit?"

"Yes, your Wood Elf males said that I would know what to bring."

We waited until Ursus's breathing evened out, telling us that he was unconscious. "Well, time to get him down. I just wonder what his partner is going to say when she sees his back." I stood up to unchain him.

"He is married, and he chose to do this? Why?! Why would he mar his body like this just to feel the pain?"

"I have lived with Wood Elves for over five years now. Trust me when I say that the males tend to forget that they are not all-powerful Gods of the forest." I put him over my shoulders and down my back to carry him. "Go ahead and get the chains undone so we can get him fixed up."

She took the chains from around his wrists, dropping him onto my back.

"We may forget that we are not forest Gods, but I know a former City Elf who forgets that she cannot take on the world without help." Howling Wolf pulled Ursus off me.

"I had him," I grumbled.

"You were about to collapse from his weight, my little Snow." He blew me a kiss, then walked to where the City Elves were.

"They are nothing like the stories say they are," the City Elf woman mumbled.

We moved to where the other Elves were. "No, they are not. That is why they need your help. City Elves don't trust Wood Elves because of those stories. They trust me even less. But if a Matriarch trusts them, then the City Elves are more likely to trust them. The Wood Elves will help teach everyone how to live out here and offer protection. In exchange, the City Elves can become a trading post and neutral territory for the Clans. It will be a lot of work, but I am hoping that one day, the City Elves will be free from their bondage forever."

"I want that, too." Her eyes became misty with tears.

"Then let us fulfill that dream, Matriarch."

"Have you heard of the Reckoning?" she asked me.

I nodded. "It is our oldest myth, a creature of the Goddess who avenges those under its protection."

"I have always wondered if there was some sort of truth to it, or if it was always a myth to give us hope during dark times," she mused out loud. "How do you get over the fear that has been ingrained in us for so long? That terror of what would happen if you got recaptured."

"I never did, truthfully. You see, I was caught after being with the Wood Elves. I thought that I would never see them again. The thing I was able to learn is that we protect our own. They found me and saved me. They could have decided that I was not worth it, or that the threat of capture was too great. They never hesitated in coming for me," I explained. "I still have nightmares and wake up in a cold sweat, thinking I was back under the humans. It took a while for the Wood Elves to convince me that my life is worth just as much as anyone else's." I opened the door.

"Is that why you have a name?" She started to work on Ursus's back, as I handed her the herbs Sparrow gave me.

"No," Howling Wolf answered her. "She has a name because she killed a bear that attacked the village."

The City Elves looked between Howling Wolf and me, their jaws dropped.

"She was given a warrior's name because of that. Normally, our females get their names when they start their yearly blood."

The Matriarch and the other City Elves flushed in embarrassment.

"Howling Wolf, it is not polite to talk about that in mixed company."

"You do with the gossip girls," he pointed out.

I raised an eyebrow at him. "Are you female? Did you grow breasts and lose a certain part of your anatomy?" He was about to answer when Ursus started to stir. "Do not move. The Matriarch is getting you fixed up, so do not move unless you want to reopen the wounds."

"This is what awaited you every time you rebelled?" Ursus whispered.

"Yes. Would you be willing to fight, knowing that the humans outnumber you and that pain is what awaits if you failed in your rebellion?" I asked.

"No, I would not." He looked at me from where the Matriarch was working. "No wonder you throw your life with reckless abandon. Glad she is yours, because I would have probably throttled her for how much she puts you through."

"Done," the Matriarch told him. "The skin is still fragile, so if you retear them open, you will scar up more than just the lash lines you will get from this."

"Then how is Snow's body covered in scars that are not just lines?" Ursus asked her while Howling Wolf and First Son helped him sit up.

"Because we started healing your back quickly. Part of the punishment is to leave the Elf hanging from the chains. And if the Elf is female..." She tried to figure out how to say it without being blunt.

I did not have that problem. "Half Elf children are rarely created from love."

The Wood Elf males stiffened at that.

"My scars are worse because every time they tried that with me; I fought them. I made sure their hands became slick with my blood. I made damned sure that every time they looked at their bed, they would see the blood they spilled. Then they would see it while they were looking to rape another Elf. Most human males cannot keep those images from their heads, so they would not use a City Elf woman that way after me." I shook the memories off. "But enough about that kind of talk. She has agreed to become the Matriarch of the City Elf settlement. So, First Son and Cristata will have to figure out how to make that happen."

"Speaking of Cristata, how are we going to explain Ursus' wounds to her?" Wolf asked me.

I put my palms out in front of me. "Do not look at me. He gets to explain it to his partner about it, since it was his idea."

"How long until he can walk?" First Son looked at the Matriarch.

"A few hours. That will also give us long enough to take any supplies the humans left," she answered, giving a silent command to a couple of the City Elves. "Speaking of them, what do we do with the bodies?"

"We leave them for the creatures of the forest. With the rain, their blood should wash away, " First Son told her.

"At least some good will come from the humans being here," the Matriarch mused.

"Besides freedom?"

She grinned, showing a sadistic side that matched mine. "The predators will be too full to worry about us."

Chapter 18

"Sparrow!" I called out.

"Sh!" She grabbed me and hid behind a building.

"What is—" She covered my mouth with her hand.

"Quiet! They will hear you!" she whispered sharply.

I used my hands to ask her who.

"First Son and Wolf. They have been sneaking around and have been very secretive lately. They are planning something."

I signed that they are always secretive because of their jobs.

"Do you know what they are planning?"

I shook my head.

"Then it has nothing to do with their work." She bit her thumb, keeping an eye on them.

I whispered, "Why do you not just ask them?"

She looked at me, shocked. "What makes you think they would tell me?"

"I know that they are planning on going up to the City Elf settlement for a couple of days with a few warriors to teach the City Elves how to protect themselves."

She jolted and grabbed my shirt. "They have been spending a lot of time up there recently. Did you not say that their Elder is a woman?"

"Not Elder. Matriarch. Age is not a factor in City Elf leaders," I corrected her.

She freaked out. "What if First Son is falling in love with her?"

"Why would he?" I asked her, hoping she could see how absurd that idea was.

"She is a strong leader. From what some of the warriors said about her, she carries an air about her that fascinates them. What if First Son finds her fascinating, too?"

"They like her because she is something new and shiny. Remember how they acted when I first got here? Same kind of thing. Once I was no longer a new toy to play with, they stopped looking at me like that."

"They leave you alone because you kept kicking their asses, then Wolf claimed you as his," she grumbled.

"Look, Sparrow. You know that this is ridiculous, correct?"

"But the warriors talk about her with awe. They say that she is delicate, but strong willed. She is beautiful with her shining light brown hair and blue eyes. How can I compete with that?"

"You do not have to. First Son—"

She covered my mouth as the two males came over, each carrying a heavy sack, "Good morning, Sparrow, Snow." First Son smiled. "What are you two up to today?"

Sparrow spoke first. "I have to help the ladies with the...washing." She practically ran away, leaving the three of us.

"What was that about? It is not a washing day."

"She is just having an off day." I looked at my friend as she escaped into the throng of Clans mates. "So, what have you two been up to?"

Howling Wolf showed me what was in his sack. "Winter is coming, so we wanted to make sure the City Elves had things to keep them warm over the cold months. The males there already know how to chop wood and make a fire, but these pelts should help them conserve their dried wood."

First Son showed me his. "I asked the gossip girls to help put together things that they think the City Elves would need to get started on making things, so they can start their trading post."

I picked up some of the different fabrics and remembered something. "You should also see if any of them have yarn, since a lot of City Elf females usually weave things in their off times. It helps pass the time faster when the nights are long. And it allows them to gossip like the gossip girls do over their cooking."

"That is a great idea! I will see if they have anything." First Son went back to the village.

Howling Wolf looked at me and grabbed my hand. He led me to a tree that the villagers planted a few years ago for me. We climbed on top of our home. "Now what did you not want him to know?"

"Sparrow is worried that the Matriarch is catching First Son's eye."

"What?" He apparently was not expecting that.

"She thinks that because the Matriarch is fascinating to many of the warriors that visit the City Elf settlement, that First Son thinks so, too. She is not listening to reason when I tried to explain that they like her because she is something different than them, just like I was. Add in that a few of the warriors are young eligible males, and I could see why they would decide to stay in the settlement to help protect it."

"My sister is an idiot sometimes."

216

"No, she is not. She is just a woman in love who does not see that First Son only has eyes for her. I just hope she does not do anything stupid that would jeopardize that. I know how she feels sometimes. Even though I know that you love me, it is hard seeing how some of the women in the village keep hoping to steal you away."

"They what?" He gaped.

"They brush up against you, touch your arm while they talk to you, ask you to help when with something they can do themselves to get your attention. If you had shown any of them anything more than the kindness that you carry, I would be in Sparrow's position. Then again, if you ever showed any inclination of wanting to be with someone new, I would step aside for them. But I know that you only have eyes for me."

I could see the wheels in his head turning, as he realized what I was talking about. "If another male tried to take you away from me, I would kick their ass in a Test of Taking."

"I remember you and First Son already did one for me that one time. What is it?"

He scowled at the rooftop, then laid back to look up to the sky. "A Test of Taking can be done whenever a male believes that another is not treating a female right. Usually, it is done when

217

two males want the chance to court a female. But in your case, he called me out on how I was treating you, as a friend of yours."

"Is there a version where two women fight to be with a male? Because I would fight off any female that tries to tumble in your bed without your explicit consent."

He laughed. "No, there is nothing like that. Females tend to be more vicious than males are when it comes to wanting a male for themselves. Your gender tends to fight dirty." He pulled me closer to him. "But I am glad to hear that you would fight for me. Especially after saying you would step aside if I wanted it. I can promise that my eyes have not nor will they ever stray from you. Do City Elves have anything like that?"

"Not really. We do not partner up like Wood Elves. We could pair up for a few years or just a night of companionship. Maybe you will decide that you want a delicate flower instead of a thorny one like me," I teased.

"But the thorns are worth being in the beauty of that flower." He kissed my temple.

I laughed. "Goddess Above, you are hopeless."

"If you two are done being lovey-dovey, Howling Wolf and I need to get the warriors to get going," First Son said from the tree. "Snow, you will oversee taking care of the village while we are gone. I have been trying to find Sparrow to tell her goodbye, but none of the gossip girls knows where she is. Since we cannot wait any longer, can you find her to make sure she is feeling well?"

Howling Wolf sat up, pulling me with him.

"I will find her," I promised. "Just be careful and come back as soon as possible. Grandfather says that the snow will be coming in early this year. As fun as it would be to dig you out, I would prefer to stay where it is warm."

"Do not stay too warm. Then I will not have a purpose when I come back." Howling Wolf grinned as he stood up, then helped me up.

"I will find a purpose for you. Now get going." I edged him toward the tree to climb down. I waved at them as they and their warriors left the village. I climbed off the roof and wandered to the kitchens. "Have you ladies seen Sparrow around?"

"We already told the First Son that we have not," Xerinae said with a bitterness in her voice.

"He is gone, and I am missing the necessary parts to take his place."

Xerinae looked at me. "She is sad."

"She is worried that First Son does not love her," I told her. "Do you have any advice on how to convince her otherwise?"

Xerinae stabbed the board she was cutting vegetables on with her knife. "Is he not treating her right?"

I put my hands up in front of me defensively. "Nothing like that. She just thinks that First Son is falling in love with the Matriarch of the City Elf settlement because she is a leader of her people, like he is."

"Is he falling in love with the Matriarch?"

"Goddess Above, no," I told her, wondering how this conversation turned so badly. "What is going on? You are not normally this snarly at me."

"Besides that Sparrow came through here crying? Some of the warriors who pronounced their love for one of the women has decided that they would rather partner with a City Elf."

"City Elves do not partner like Wood Elves do. Why would anyone throw away a lifetime together for a short time of pleasure?"

"You tell us."

I was surrounded by the angry looks from the gossip girls. "I will see what I can find out. Get me a list of those who left and their partners, and how long they were together. Also, write down a brief explanation about partnerships for Wood Elves and what it means. Give it to Grandfather, and I will collect it from him. Just please tell Sparrow that she has nothing to worry about. First Son loves her with everything he is. His eyes are not going to stray just because something shiny and new is there." With that, I escaped from the kitchen and said to myself, "No wonder Sparrow is worried."

I found a couple of the warriors who I trusted, Lynx and Raven, and dragged to a nearby building, where I pushed them into chairs. "Tell me about how Wood Elves court each other. Then explain about what happens when one partner wants out of the partnership."

They looked at each other and Raven finally asked, "Is something wrong?"

"You are damned right there is something wrong. Get to explaining." I crossed my arms over my chest, waiting.

"As you have seen, we have different festivals where males and females can explore their different options. Courtships take years, sometimes decades, as both Elves try to decide if that person is the Elf they want to spend their life with. By normal Wood Elf standards, you and Howling Wolf moved quickly, but that is also because you both spent almost every waking moment together," Raven started.

"What happens when they decide that they found the right person?" I asked.

Lynx answered, "Then those two people go in front of the Elder and Grandfather to announce their intentions to handfast for ten years. They live together, acting as they would if they were partners. Think of it as a final test to be absolutely sure about their partnership. After that, we have a celebration, where they tell the entire village about their partnership, where they become official."

"What happens if someone wants out at any point?"

"Up until it is official, either can back out without consequences. After becoming official, they become ostracized by the Clan. Most times, they end up leaving to join another Clan during times of peace. We take our partnerships extremely seriously. That is why if there's any hint of mistreatment, someone can call a Test of Taking. Usually, it snaps the male out of whatever problem they are causing."

"What is the female equivalent to a Test of Taking?"

Raven shook his head. "There is none. Males can do it because women are naturally weaker than us when it comes to strength. Now, if a male feels like he is being mistreated, then we talk to the women who speak to the offending woman, and she fixes her behavior."

"If someone does not change what they are doing?"

"Then we get the Elder and Grandfather involved. If they get involved, it never turns out well for the offender. But like we said earlier, usually a Test of Taking will make the male realize what he would be losing, so they change."

"City Elves do not have their own traditions about love?" Lynx asked me.

I shook my head. "No, we do not. We never had that privilege of being with someone for too long. City Elves are bought and sold so quickly, that it is hard to make those kinds of connections. Instead, we might spend some nights with a companion, but it never goes passed that. The humans say that we cannot love at all. So, this is all new territory for me. Thank you for taking the time to explain it to me." Knowing all of this made me angrier at the warriors who were leaving their partners.

"Is everything fine, Snow?" Raven asked.

"No, it is not." I felt the Snow Cat take over involuntarily. "Everything is not well, Raven." I left them there, stomping my way toward Grandfather's building. Anyone who came close to

223

me, stepped out of the way when they saw my eyes. Elves whispered and mumbled, but I ignored them. I went inside the building and paced back and forth, wanting to try to calm down. It did not help. Footsteps resounded near me, and I snarled at whoever was breaking my stride.

Grandfather hesitated, never giving him the full force of the Snow Cat's rage. He set the tea on the table next to me. "The ladies gave me a letter that they said you were waiting for." He set the paper next to the tea. "Mind telling me what has made you so angry, Silent Snow?"

I snatched the paper and opened it, growling louder with each name. I looked at the older Elf, trying to pull back from wanting to tear something apart. "Broken promises and those who make them. Broken hearts and those who tore them apart."

He stiffened.

"I am going to the City Elf settlement; Raven is in charge."

"Stay safe, Silent Snow," Grandfather said as I walked out the door.

I ran into the forest, trying to burn off the rage I felt. I did not see the forest or the animals that lived there. I was too focused on the betrayal and hurt of my gossip girls.

"How dare they break their commitment..."

City Elves never got the chance to love, so seeing these idiots throw it away for a short time of passion just made me angrier.

I ran into the City Elf settlement, just to see Lynx already there. He was talking with Howling Wolf and First Son, probably to warn them that I was on the warpath.

Howling Wolf ran over to me. "Snow, what is goin—"

"I need to see the warriors." My voice was deadly calm.

"Not until you talk to me." He put his hand on my shoulder.

I dropped my shoulder and moved out of the way. "If you will not get them, I will, Enforcer." I used his title, knowing full well that it created a separation from personal lives and our duties. He did not look at me, as he left to grab the Wood Elves from our Clan. When he gathered them all, and I looked at them. Some were fearful because they had never been on that side of the Snow Cat, they shook, and their eyes widened. Others looked annoyed at being pulled away from whatever they were doing.

The Matriarch came up to me. "Snow?" She saw my eyes and changed her tactics. "What can I do for you, Enforcer?"

I handed her the list of names and explained.

She opened it, and her eyes widened as she read. "I did not know, Enforcer." Her voice was quiet, but I heard the simmering anger under it. She pointed them out to me. "Those of you who I call out will stay, the rest of you will go back to work," she told them. As she called out their names, the pattern emerged.

"What is—" First Son tried to ask, but both the glare from the Matriarch and I stopped his question.

"Matriarch, you explain to the City Elves about this. I will explain a few things to these Wood Elves."

"Of course, Enforcer. I will be sure to tell the City Elves everything." She went toward where the City Elves were watching.

I grabbed my daggers and threw them at the feet of the Elves who strayed from their partnerships. "I challenge all of you to a Test of Taking."

Some took a step back, not sure what to do. Howling Wolf, First Son, and Lynx looked at me, then to the warriors who were standing there.

"Under what circumstances?" one of them asked.

"For hurting those under my protection. Each of you has decided to break your partnership by trying to stay here. You betrayed your partners like the wayward idiots you are. Under those circumstances, I challenge all of you. If you believe that you are worthy of the love that your partners have given you, without asking for anything but yours in return... If you believe you are worthy of being allowed to remain in the good graces of the women you hurt..." I looked at all of them. "Then you take this as your final warning. If you decide that you will break your partnership, then I will make sure that every person in the Clan and our allies know about your wandering eyes."

The Matriarch returned. "This place is off limits to those who choose to break their vows."

"Therefore, you will have nowhere to go, unless you think that you can defeat me in the Test of Taking." My voice was a little louder than a growl.

None of the males moved; the Matriarch handed me back the names and letter. "My people have been told about you breaking your vows to someone you love and chose to spend your life with. None of them knew about you having a partner waiting for you at home. They have decided that if you try to bed them again, they will make sure that you will not survive the experience. We are not to be used again."

"A City Elf thinking they can kill a Wood Elf warrior? I doubt that. I will kill any City Elf that tries to raise a blade to me. As for my bitch of a partner, I could not care less about her." The same voice who asked about the circumstances came forward. He was a newcomer from another Clan, accepted along with his partner into the village.

"Enough, Viper," Howling Wolf warned.

"If he thinks he can hurt me, he can try. But if he does try, I will kill him." I glanced at the Matriarch, a sadistic smile on my face. "Should you tell him about the City Elf protector, or should I?"

"I think you will better get the point through than I could, Enforcer." She returned my smile, and I saw Howling Wolf, First Son, and Lynx shudder from the looks we passed between us.

I retrieved my daggers from the ground and said, "City Elves have our myths and traditions, just like Wood Elves do. Except ours are grounded in blood." I stood ready for the newcomer to attack me like he was itching to do.

The other City Elves made symbols of protection on their chests.

"Come and get me if you think you can. Hell, I will even grant you a boon if you win."

"Fine." Viper shrugged. "If I win, I get the Matriarch to use as I please." He raised up his short sword, reminding me of the ones humans carried.

I became cold inside as they did when killing the humans and slavers.

"One of the myths told through the ages spoke of a powerful force. Darkness and evil were coming for the Goddess's children," the Matriarch explained to Howling Wolf, First Son, and Lynx.

Viper launched himself at me, hoping for a quick victory. He and I never sparred, so he had no idea how I fought.

I ducked under his wild strike, as I slashed up at his arm, nothing that would stop him from fighting.

The Matriarch's sing-song voice gave the myth life. "Where do I begin? The Goddess sent Her children someone who could protect them."

He slashed down, so I dodged to the side, adding a couple more cuts to his skin.

She continued, "That protector was raised through pain and death, bathing in the blood of its enemies. Those enemies paid for their sins with their lives. The protector was the reaper outside of their door; when they took everything, it got what it came for. Like the sound of all the stars, crashing in the dark, the Goddess said a prayer and buried its name. Up through the ashes, it rose like wildfire."

He kept trying to slash and stab me, but I just kept dodging out of the way, slicing through his flesh. He was slowing down, but I was speeding up. I kept just lightly cutting him, just enough to draw a little bit of blood.

"You see, they got what they gave, when they took their last breath, as they were laid to rest. The Goddess gave this protector a name that we would wait to hear again, as it was the name of our salvation from slavery."

I backed away from Viper, waiting for him to attack me one last time.

"What was the protector's name?" Lynx asked. His voice sound distant.

There was a glint in the Matriarch's eyes, as Viper attacked me again. He tried slashing from overhead, coming down on me. I moved up right into his face, and there was intense fear and terror in his eyes.

I answered Lynx, "It was named the Reckoning, and it used twin blades as its weapon."

I stabbed into Viper's stomach and slashed my daggers opposite ways, cutting through the spongy part of the ribs and down through the soft organs, hitting the artery in his thigh. I ripped my daggers out of him, crossing them in front of his throat. I waited until his throat touched the center of the crossed blades, pulling them apart, cutting his throat almost to his spine. I moved out of the way; his body fell to the ground.

"That protector is why all City Elves are taught how to use knives, even if we have to use proxy weapons, because the humans would not let us have real ones." She smiled at me. "The first time I saw you with your daggers, it felt like the myth came to life. Then we talked about freeing the other City Elves... and I knew that even if you were not our sacred protector from the Goddess, I believed that you became the Reckoning."

I cleaned my daggers on Viper's torn clothes. "I have no illusions of grandeur like that. Truthfully, I am sure that any other Elf could do what I do with enough practice."

It was like the spell of the Matriarch's voice broke with me talking.

Howling Wolf looked at Viper on the ground. "He said he came to our Clan to rebuild his life. What do we tell his partner?"

"I bet if you talk to his partner, you will find out the truth. This doesn't feel like the first time he has acted like that," the Matriarch told him. "As for what we tell his partner, we tell her the truth. He died in battle. She does not need to hear about his view of her." She looked to the First Son. Since you are the leader of the warriors, that task falls on you. Do not be surprised if she looks more relieved than sad."

She then looked to the males who had chosen to break their partnerships. "I suggest you all go home and beg for forgiveness from your partners. Get ready to work to earn their trust back. If I learn that any of you stray again, you will see that Snow is not the only City Elf who knows how to wield a knife. Now, go get your things and leave." We waited until the straying males did as she commanded, the City Elf males escorting them.

Howling Wolf walked over to me, pointing at Viper's body. "This is why there is no Test of Taking for women. I do not like that you killed a fellow Clan member, but I understand why you did. If the Matriarch is correct about his partner being relieved, then it becomes more justified."

He looked to the Matriarch. "What would you have done if she lost?"

"Do you trust the Goddess? Because I do. And the Goddess gifted City Elves with wiles, viciousness, and dirty tricks, while She gave Wood Elves honor, family, and love. I am done being used by those who think they can control me. He would not have survived the night."

"Goddess Above, I hope all City Elf females are not like you two," First Son mumbled a prayer. "What started this whole thing?"

"Sparrow is worried that you are falling in love with the Matriarch."

He choked. "What?!" He looked to the Matriarch. "No offense given, but you are not my type."

She just laughed. "None taken. You are too tall at the minimum I do not know how your neck does not hurt when talking to these tall males."

"The women are almost just as tall, maybe only six feet instead of six and a half."

"Goddess Above." She laughed, before waving to me. "Always a pleasure, Snow."

Lynx ran over to her, offering his arm to escort her. She accepted it, and they walked away, leaving First Son, Howling Wolf, and I next to Viper's body.

233

"You were saying about Sparrow?" First Son prompted.

"She thought you were falling for the Matriarch, and she would not listen to me that you love only her. Then after you two left, Xerinae snarled at me, and that is how I learned about the straying males. I had Raven and Lynx explain the whole partnership thing to me, and when they were done, I was even more furious." I thought about. "Speaking of Lynx, he must have left the village right after our talk. What were you three talking about when I got here?"

"Lynx and Raven thought that there was something wrong between us because you never explained that there was something wrong from your ladies." He looked to the body on the ground. "We cannot leave him here."

"No, but we could leave him near a bear den," I offered. When they both arched an eyebrow at my suggestions, I said, "Fine. Maybe in the river, so he can sleep with the fishes."

"Your ideas are useless, Snow." Howling Wolf touched my shoulders, and he jumped back, looking at the blood on them. "How much of that is yours?"

"None? He did not land any hits on me, because he was swinging too wildly."

"Go to the bathhouse and get cleaned up," he grumbled, pushing me away from the body.

I walked to the bathhouse. The City Elves who helped to build up this settlement wanted something of comfort. I remembered bathhouses from the cities, but this one was simpler. The area they chose had a natural hot spring in it, so they built the wooden structure over it, adding in decking and partitioned rooms. The City Elf running it waved me through, as he grabbed me a scour pad and a drying cloth. I stripped out of the bloody clothes and went to where the buckets were. I used the dipper to pour the water over me, warmed by the hot spring's heat. When I finished scrubbing the blood off me, threw my clothes into the bucket to soak.

I climbed into the hot spring, letting its heat help my muscles. The Matriarch came in, carrying her own supplies. She cleaned herself, before sitting next to me. "What a day."

"Sorry for getting blood all over your village." I laid my head back on the cool stone.

"Do not worry about it. That bastard got what he deserved." After a moment, she asked, "Snow? Are we really going to try to liberate the City Elves?"

My brows furrowed. "I may live with Wood Elves, but I am a City Elf. I want our people free. I want them to experience what the Goddess Above has given us in the world. I want them to never have to live in fear again."

"I have an idea that can help with getting them wanting to escape again."

I turned to face her. "What are you thinking?"

"We were always able to get stories passed along because of how often we were bought and sold. I want to use that to our advantage. I want to spread a rumor around that the Reckoning has returned, and she has silver hair. I know you do not believe that you are that special, but no one can handle the knives like you can. I could train for the rest of my life and never reach your level. Beyond that, even if it is just a hope, it is more than what we have ever had. Then, when you liberate them, they will be more likely to run when you tell them to."

"It will be extremely dangerous. I cannot ask my Clan to do this with me."

"What will be dangerous?" Howling wolf walked in with First Son and Lynx.

The Matriarch looked at me, her face flushed with embarrassment. I waited until they were in the water before I said anything. "You know, as lovely as your physique is, Howling Wolf, I do believe our Matriarch is embarrassed since she got an eyeful."

"It is payback for you two scaring us earlier," Lynx mumbled. He turned to the Matriarch. "You just watched someone eviscerate another Elf. How can someone so cute and little be so vicious?"

"It is because they are closer to the Underworld at their height." Howling Wolf sounded solemn. "As for the cute part, I am starting to believe that the Goddess Above had a sense of humor when She made City Elves."

I elbowed the Matriarch. "They think you are cute." I got in close to her ear and whispered, "According to the ladies, Lynx is a catch. And he is more of your type."

She grabbed me and dunked me into the water and held me there for a couple seconds. "I am so sorry, Wolf. Your lady just mysteriously drowned. Just happened out of nowhere."

"Oh no, what ever will I do?" Howling Wolf asked sarcastically.

I pushed her under the water. "Lynx, she thinks you are good looking, even if she will not admit it." I pulled her back out of the water and hid behind Howling Wolf.

"So, what is this dangerous thing that my Snow is trying to avoid talking about with her antics?" Howling Wolf asked again.

The Matriarch answered, a glittering fire behind her eyes, "Liberating the City Elves."

Chapter 19

"Let me get this straight, Silent Snow killed a new Clan member because you believed him to have harmed female Elves before, and he broke his vows to his partner. Then, you two decided that you two want to liberate the City Elves from their servitude without the help of your Clan or allies?" the Elder asked me.

"Correct, Honorable Elder," the Matriarch told him. "We are not asking for your Clan to put your warriors at risk for something like this, nor are we asking for this to happen immediately. This is too important to her and myself to push it to the wayside, so I am asking permission to use her when the time comes. We will take our time to plan, letting the rumor of the return of the Reckoning to spread throughout the kingdom. City Elves have already waited for so long, so taking the time to make sure that we keep our people safe while we save others is paramount."

The Elder and Grandfather looked between the Matriarch and me. "You asked to be a part of this Clan, and now you are willing to throw it all away for those who believe you to be a Kinkiller?"

"Yes, Honorable Elder," I replied to him. "I may live here, but I will always be something separate from them because of what I am. I love this Clan with everything I am and will die to protect it, but I wonder. What will happen when the humans run out of City Elves to buy and sell, then kill for their entertainment? Would they try to go after Wood Elves next? Liberating the City Elves has the advantage to make sure that the Wood Elves are never on the slave block."

He looked at me.

Grandfather spoke. "Do you believe humans would be so foolish as to try to capture the Wood Elves for slavery?"

"If there is anything that I learned in my three thousand years on this earth, it is that humans are foolish and haughty. I believe it is only a matter of time before they try. There are more humans than there are Elves, so if they decided that Wood Elves would make good slaves, they can overcome us with their sheer numbers. We need to make sure that the laws are changed so that slavery is abolished completely, but that will not happen without help from other Clans or even human allies."

The Elder scoffed. "Humans as allies?"

I looked to the Matriarch, who nodded and spoke. "I know of a family who has purchased City Elves throughout their

240

generations, but never treated them badly. Every time an Elf went to a slave auction, we hoped that they would be the ones to purchase us. At least, they would help give us the semblance of freedom, even if, by law, they were not able to release us. I believe this family will help us in liberating our people."

"I cannot force my Clan nor other Clans into assisting you, Matriarch," the Elder said. "But if Silent Snow volunteers to help, I know better than to try to stop her."

"Thank you, Honorable Elder." She gave him a graceful bow, "May I inquire about those Clans who you consider allies, so I may ask their Elders directly?"

"You want to speak to unknown Clan Elders about something they would never have considered doing?"

"Yes," she answered simply.

He looked to Howling Wolf and First Son. "It seems City Elf females are bred to have gumption and grit."

"That sounds about right, Father," First Son told him. "Maybe their fortitude can help us, where their wiles cannot. We all know how cunning Snow is, but I am starting to see a pattern with other City Elf females."

"I believe you have a map that she can use?" the Elder asked Grandfather.

Grandfather pulled out the map of the allies, enemies, and neutrals against our Clan. "Please, take a look, Matriarch."

The Matriarch stepped forward and looked at the map. "Who would you suggest I speak with first? We already have the Star Clan's pledge to assist, after they first saved my people."

"Might I suggest that you try the Earth Clan? They are neutral toward us, so they would not mind you having an escort with you." Grandfather pointed.

She studied the map, looking for routes in and out of the village in case she needed to escape quickly. "May I take Lynx with me? Since he is the fastest scout, if something goes wrong, he would be able to get help."

"I am surprised you did not want to take Silent Snow with you." Grandfather chuckled.

"If I was going to fight, I would. But since this is a peace mission, I would rather not come with an Enforcer. Sorry, Snow."

I laughed. "I completely understand your reasoning. I would not want me for something that delicate either. But if something does go wrong, do not think you can try to stop me from saving you." I pointed to the Elder, then Grandfather,

Howling Wolf, then First Son, "Only they would be able to, and I am sure Howling Wolf would be there leading the way."

"You may take Lynx with you. I suggest waiting until tomorrow morning before leaving, so you have enough supplies," the Elder told her.

"Thank you, Honorable Elder." She gave him a bow of respect, before leaving.

I tried to follow, but the Elder stopped me. "Tell me everything that happened yesterday."

I took a deep breath and started with Sparrow's worry, the talking with my gossip girls, then the Test of Taking, followed by killing Viper.

"When First Son told Viper's partner about his death, she thanked him. When the gossip girls got her to talk, they learned that he had raped another Elf in their previous Clan and left her for dead. She was found alive, but Viper had already taken his partner here. He beat her whenever he had what he considered a bad day, which could range from stubbing his toe in the morning to her not giving him sex on demand." I bristled with rage. "I wish she would have opened up sooner, so we could have helped her sooner."

"Knowing more about this helps me understand why you killed him." Grandfather sounded empty since he and the Elder had given permission for Viper and his partner. "Would you mind finding out if his partner would prefer to return to her former Clan or stay here? She will not pay for the sins of her dead partner."

"The gossip girls already asked, and she would like to stay. He beat her so badly that she actually believed that she could have stopped him from hurting that other woman if she wasn't such a terrible partner," I told them. "I am asking permission to go to their former Clan to explain Viper's death. It will not give them the revenge they want, nor will it take away the pain he caused the woman, but it will help her heal."

"I grant permission. Take Raven with you, since he is a better negotiator than you are. Howling Wolf, I want you to stay here with First Son, since I believe we will be having visitors coming after dealing with the Matriarch," The Elder told the others. "You are all dismissed."

"Yes, Honorable Elder." We all bowed before leaving the large building.

"When did you decide to go to their former village?" Howling Wolf asked me.

"After talking with the gossip girls. They pretty much demanded that someone go, because of what Viper's partner told them. I decided I should because I know what the woman he raped is going through. I want to be the one to tell her that it gets better, and she will heal from this."

First Son stopped us. "I remember you telling us, and we saw about a few of them. And I know that is never a good thing to ask, but how often are City Elf women forced into a bed?"

I looked at him, appraising if he would be able to handle the answer, before replying, "It depends, honestly. Me? At least three times a week, because of how rare I was to them. Too many kept trying to breed, so they would get a silver haired Half Elf. Whether it was luck or the Goddess Above, the pregnancy never caught. For other City Elves? Once a week, usually. You see, it was not just the masters who sexually abused the slaves, and the men were not exempt from it either. There are poisons that can make a male physically ready, but it still does not change the horror of what was done to them."

"Goddess Above." First Son looked sick.

"It is amazing that any of you let someone else touch you at all, much less have sex," Howling Wolf mumbled.

"You learn to disassociate when you are forced, just like we do when we get hurt. As for sex with other City Elves, we all know what triggers harmful memories, so we all know how to avoid them with each other. It is another reason we cannot love someone else because love requires giving yourself to that person in its entirety. We are unable to do that, which is another reason why I was so angry at the wandering males." I clenched my fists. "Wood Elves have the ability to love and form lifelong partnerships, whereas we cannot."

First Son rubbed his chin. "I wonder if time heals soul wounds as it does other ones, because maybe after you liberate the City Elves, and they have the chance to heal, then they could have the ability to love."

"I never thought of that before. I have been here for over five years, but that is such a short time in an Elf's life. Maybe you are right, and we could learn to feel what you do." I caught Sparrow walking towards her home. "Speaking of love." I ran to her and dragged her to where First Son and Howling Wolf were. "Tell her."

First Son cocked his head; Howling Wolf coughed, "Tell her how you feel."

There was finally the glimmer of understanding in his eyes. "Sparrow." He grabbed her hands, and I dragged Howling Wolf away to give them privacy.

"If City Elves cannot love, then what do you feel for me?" Howling Wolf asked.

"What I feel for you is the closest thing to love I can experience, which is respect and admiration, which is why I told you that if you wanted another, I would step aside. But I do not feel the same way you do, and there is a chance I never will be able to."

He picked me up his hands under my hips, to lift me to his level. He pressed his forehead to mine. "What we have is enough for me, Snow. Even if you never love me the way I do you, the fact is that we chose each other. You could have very easily gone with any of the other warriors or even stayed an eligible, but when you learned how I felt, you chose to be with me. If that is not love, then I guess none of us know what love truly is."

I smiled at him then laughed. "I doubt any of the other warriors would appreciate my ability to throw them into the dirt like you do, so that counted almost all of them out anyways."

The Matriarch cleared her throat near us. "As adorable as you two are, I need to speak with Snow before she leaves."

Howling Wolf kissed me gently then set me back on the ground. "I will go get Raven and tell him about your mission."

The Matriarch whistled. "They may not be Gods of the Forest, but their muscles sure do help with the illusion that they are."

I gave her a friendly punch in the arm. "Go find your own Forest God. I mean Lynx is not as muscular, but I doubt that bothers you as much."

She tinted pink as she linked her arm in mine. "Lynx is a Forest God, just a leaner one, instead of the thick muscles of your Wolf."

"Besides talking about their lovely physiques, what did you need to talk to me about?" I changed the subject.

"I want you to see if you can convince the Clan you are going to visit to become a part of our cause. If I am the only one who is trying to get all the Clans to help, then it would take too long. So, I am hoping that you can help split the duties. It would be best if we could get the Clans we talk with to spread the word of our beg for assistance," she explained while we wandered.

"I will see what I can do. Maybe we could get these other Clans to spread our wishes to their allies. Especially if they know that Wood Elves have a chance to be a part of the menu, so to speak." I thought about it. "I wonder if there have been any Clans who lost people already."

"Do you think we would have heard about it?"

"I do not know, but we can also spread that if Wood Elves have been taken, to send word here and to your settlement. Maybe we could broker alliances if we are able to save them."

"Goddess Above, I hope we do not have to gain alliances that way. No matter how much easier it would be, I do not wish slavery on anyone." She made a sign of protection to the Goddess over her heart.

"Me either." Then I added, "Except for people like Viper or the City Elf Seller who first enslaved me."

Out of nowhere, Raven came up to us. "Howling Wolf told me that you and I are going on a mission? Then First Son gave me an alliance document of the Water Clan decided to accept it."

"Yes." I pulled my arm away from the Matriarch and gave her a devilish grin, pointing to a home near where we were standing. "I believe your lean Forest God has today as a rest day, if you want to spend time with him." I winked, and she punched me in the arm. "Good luck, Matriarch."

"You as well, Reckoning." She waved before walking away.

"What was that about?" Raven took a sip from his waterskin.

"She wants to bed Lynx," I told him.

He choked on the water he was drinking. "What? Is she the reason Lynx has been daydreaming since yesterday?" He put his waterskin into his back bag.

"Could be. She likes his lean muscles, and the fact he is not as tall as the rest of you. She might even like talking with him, since she asked that he escort her to the Earth Clan's village."

He laughed as we left the Moon Clan's village. We walked through the forest in companionable silence, just listening to the forest life before they bed down for the winter.

"Do you think it will start snowing soon?" he asked.

"I hope not. I would rather be back in our own village before anything hits." I gave him a sly look. "And I am sure Xerinae wants you back as well, or she will get too cold at night."

"She radiates heat like the cooking fires, so if anything, she warms my bed."

"I will make sure she hears about that," I teased him.

"I will toss you into the river, if you do," he teased back. "Then again, you might like that because then you get to snuggle up to Wolf even more."

We entered the Water Clan's territory, the former Clan of Viper and his partner. We kept our hands away from our weapons, so they knew we were not a threat. Warriors came down to us. "Why are you here?"

I spoke up. "We bring news for a woman in your village. I will only speak to the woman who was raped by a warrior named Viper."

The lead warrior looked between the two of us, then motioned his men to grab us.

I pushed the Snow Cat down, not wanting to fight yet.

"Does this City Elf speak for you? Why does she wear the clothes of the Moon Clan's Enforcer?" He looked to Raven.

"She is our Enforcer's Second, as such I defer to her. We are not here to cause trouble. We only want to deliver news then return home."

The lead warrior reassessed me. "This tiny creature is the Moon Clan Enforcer's Second? How can that be?"

I smiled. "It had to be my cute looks and tiny demeanor."

Raven scowled. "Let us deliver our message, and she might give you a demonstration on how she became that rank."

"The woman will not want to talk to you about Viper," he said.

My voice went cold. "I do not need for her to talk about him. I need her to listen to how he died at my hands."

"She killed him?" The lead warrior looked between Raven and me.

"From what I was told, she tore him apart," Raven told him.

The lead warrior turned to his warriors. "Bring them. The Elder will know what to do."

They bound our hands with rope and led us to their village. I had to run a few times to keep up with their ground-eating steps. One of the warriors ended up just picking me up because I kept falling behind. We entered a village that looked like our own when the warrior dropped me onto the ground. I rolled and popped back up, grateful Howling Wolf worked with me on that.

The Elder, a woman, came out of her large building. "What did you bring?"

"Two members of the Moon Clan, Honorable Elder. The City Elf claims she killed Viper, while the Moon Clan warrior agrees with her," the lead warrior told her.

"Come forward, City Elf."

I stepped up to the Elder but kept far enough away to make sure the warriors would not get antsy. "Yes, Honorable Elder?"

"Did you kill Viper?"

"Yes, Honorable Elder, though I killed him before I knew that he raped someone. I wish to talk with the woman, so she knows how he died. I also want to give assistance to her to help her heal." I moved the thick black leather and Snow Cat pelt to show her my scars. She walked up and touched them gently. "I know what she has been through, so I came here to give her peace in knowing that he will never harm another," I told the Elder in a soft voice.

She removed her fingers from my skin and touched my face. "If I sense any trickery, I will have my warriors tear your Wood Elf apart, before killing you."

"There is no trickery, Honorable Elder." I kept my eyes soft, so she would know I was not lying.

"Bring me, Bunny," she told one of her warriors. "Do you know how Blood memory magic works?"

"Yes, Honorable Elder. Our Grandfather has used it so I could show him what he needed to know."

"Bring the Moon Clan warrior with us." She looked back to me. "Follow me, and if your hands go near the daggers at your hips, we will kill you."

"Understood," I replied and followed her into the large building. There was a fire roaring, just like the one Grandfather had. I stood as far away from the large fire as I could, still uneasy about flames.

"Grandfather, we need you," she called out to an older male.

Their Grandfather was younger than ours, almost the same age as their Elder. "How may I serve you, Elder?"

"She claims to have killed Viper. I want confirmation of that." She saw me standing far away from the fire. "Why are you scared of it? Could it be because you are lying to us?"

I shook my head. "Nothing like that, Honorable Elder."

Raven came into the building, along with a woman who was younger than I was.

I felt my anger rise, seeing her. "My last master burned the City Elves alive before I was able to kill him. I could not save them all, so I do not like large fires," I told her the truth. "But you just need my blood, so you can take it from me, but I cannot get any closer to the flames."

She looked at me, her eyes hard, before she looked to the Grandfather. "Take her blood." She then looked to the shaking woman, who looked for a way to escape. "Bunny, this City Elf claims that she killed Viper. Are you willing to see his death?"

The woman shook even worse but nodded. I just wanted to hug the pain out of her, but I knew better than to move.

The Grandfather came up to me, and I offered my hands for him to cut. I thought of killing Viper as he sliced my finger. He tossed the blood into the fire and the smell of it burning made me sick. "Show us the death of Viper," the Grandfather commanded me.

I let them see me coming into the City Elf settlement and everything that came after until after Viper's death. A few of the warriors looked sick, seeing me disembowel someone. The woman's eyes were wide, as she watched and stared at the smoke memory. I then showed her how I learned of her rape, not hiding the rage I felt about it.

Raven stared, never having seen me kill like that before. "Goddess Above, Snow. That was worse than what Lynx described." He turned to the lead warrior. "That is why she is our Enforcer's Second."

I looked to the Elder. "May I speak with Bunny without the males here?"

She nodded, mollified that I had not been lying. "Release him and take him outside," she told her warriors, who all left, leaving the Elder, Grandfather, Bunny, and I alone. The Elder undid my bindings, then asked Grandfather to go make some tea.

I stepped up closer to Bunny and sat down next to her. "I am sorry for what that bastard put you through. I wanted you to see that he died a horrible death, even if it was not as slow as I wished it was. I wanted to bleed him out completely, so his pain would last. But I knew my Enforcer would not allow it."

I took off the Snow Cat pelt, black leathers, and my top, showing her my scars. She and the Elder gasped loudly, so I put my top back on. "You went through something not many Wood Elves have gone through, so you feel like you are an outcast. I know the pain you are feeling. The worry that any time someone is near you that they are going to attack you. The terror you face when you are alone at night, just before the nightmares come. The constant looking over your shoulder, wondering if anyone else is planning to harm you like he did."

She cried, "When does it stop?"

I took a deep breath, wondering if a lie would be better, but decided that she deserved the truth. "It does not stop. You learn to live with it. Some of the things start to fade, but without help, they never go away. All City Elves are raped multiple times in their lives, so we learned that talking with those who have been through what we have helps. Keeping it inside creates a festering wound, instead of letting it heal correctly. The more you accept what happened, telling someone you trust everything, and understanding that none of what he did to you is your fault, you can start to heal."

I took her hands in mine. "It is a long road, but you are not a victim, because you are a survivor. You will get through this part of your life. Your Elder and Grandfather and Clan are here for you, just as my City Elf brethren were there for me. Let them help you, Bunny, because if you try to keep it locked inside, it will tear you apart."

She fell apart.

I grabbed onto her and held her, giving her comfort.

257

After a while, she pulled away, wiping her tears. "I do not know if I am as strong as you are."

"You are stronger than you believe, but that strength does not come from fighting, instead it comes from going through a horrifying experience. I am only strong because I knew I could rely on those closest to me. Without them, I would have killed myself years ago."

She startled at that confession. "Truly?"

I nodded. "When I was found by the Moon Clan, I was ready to throw my life away, so I kept trying to find ways where I could die for something, instead of killing myself outright. I was too much of a coward of the Goddess's wrath at taking my own life, I sought out ways to die. I even fought a Bear, not caring if it killed me. I was a willing sacrifice myself to a battle against another Clan. Every time, the Dark Consort refuses to let me lie down and die. I am here today because He refused to let me kill myself." I gave her a soft smile. "Is there anyone here you can talk to and open up about what happened?"

She nodded. "My sister."

"I would also suggest talking to your Elder, since she will be able to make sure that nothing like this happens again," I told her.

"Thank you..." she said quietly, her voice trailing.

"My name is Silent Snow, but my friends just call me Snow. If at any point in time where you need to write to someone to help get your feelings out, you can write to me," I offered. "Sometimes writing is easier than trying to say the words that need to be said."

She nodded. "Thank you for everything, Snow." She wiped away her tears as she turned to her Elder. "Thank you for letting me see his death and letting me talk to her."

The Elder smiled. "Anything to help you heal, Bunny. Will you be alright to let Grandfather and I speak to Silent Snow alone?"

Bunny nodded before she got up and left.

I stood up and walked to where the Grandfather sat.

The Elder sat first. "Is it as bad as you say it is?"

I nodded to her, before taking a sip from the tea the Grandfather offered me. "Yes, but worse. I did not lie to Bunny about being raped multiple times, and you saw the scars on my body." I set the cup down on the table. "It is actually another reason I am here. The Matriarch of the City Elf settlement within our and the Star Clan's territories has asked me to speak with you about something." She looked like she was going to argue, but I stopped her. "I am not asking that you put your Clan in danger. I will not even let my Clan be put into danger. I may be willing to die for the City Elves being free, but I will not ask that of others."

"What do you want?" Grandfather asked me.

"All we want is information right now. We believe that the humans may try to capture Wood Elves when they realize that there are no more free City Elves left. We need to know if there have been any rumors or reports of such. Also, we are requesting assistance in spreading the word, so that if anyone knows anything to tell us. We would like help to liberate our people, but I cannot ask for that if anyone. The Matriarch will, though." A murderous fire rose in me. "I would also like any information you have about Clans that are a part of the slave trade."

"I will keep an ear out for anything of what you are looking for, and I will ask my allies to do the same. But, like you said, I will not ask them or my own warriors to fight for people who they do not wish to." The Elder gave me a little of what we needed.

"I thank you, Honorable Elder, for helping us."

"Might I inquire what your plans are for those who are a part of the slave trade?" Grandfather asked.

I let the Snow Cat's eyes show as a wicked smile blossomed on my lips. "I will give them a choice: help stop the slave trade or let the rivers and streams run red with their blood." I blinked a second time, the Snow Cat's eyes becoming my own again.

The Elder shuddered. "We will send along that information as we get it as well. We will warn our allies who might have ties to the slave trade to cease their actions, or they might not live to see another season."

I stood up and bowed. "I gratefully accept anything and everything you can give me, Honorable Elder. In return for your assistance, if you need anything, the Moon Clan will be there to help. Raven has the alliance document if you are willing to accept it." I bowed again, grabbed my pelt and thick black leathers, and headed outside. I whistled since it carried further than my voice could. Then I listened for its matching whistle, following it to where I found Raven sparring with a couple of the warriors.

They caught me watching and stopped.

"Raven, the Elder and Grandfather will need to look over the alliance document to decide if they want to become allies."

He dried the sweat from his skin with a cloth from a bucket. "I would ask you to take it, but you still have Snow Cat close to the surface."

"How care you tell?" I asked him, confused.

"I have been working with you for a few years now. Any of our Clan knows when you are still riding the edge between you and the Snow Cat." He grabbed his bag with the documents. "Please do not scare them too much." He smiled as he passed by me, ruffling my short hair.

I brushed my fingers through it to get it back to normal.

The lead warrior asked, "What did he mean by Snow Cat?"

I stepped under the arena fence and blinked, turning my eyes blue. "Many years ago, I met with the spirit of a Snow Cat, who agreed to merge with me in exchange for killing the human that killed her and her kittens. That human did not survive that night. As time passed, we worked together to kill other humans who we deemed as disposable, because of their crimes against City Elves." I blinked again, the Snow Cat going back into her den. "She is the reason I can move so quickly when I fight. Want to spar?"

He looked at me, apprising me from what he saw in my memory. "Why not? I am always willing to test myself against new opponents."

I took off the back bag, thick leathers, and my daggers, so I would not lose them. Then I grabbed two short sparring sticks and held them like I do my knives. "Ready when you are."

He held a single long stick. He came at me, and I used the two smaller sticks to block his attack. He was not on the same level as many of the Moon Clan warriors, and I realized why my Clan had its reputation as being vicious. I kept it light, hoping to extend the sparring session. Soon, we were both covered in sweat, despite the winter air. Raven's whistle flittered through the air, so I decided to end the match. I rushed up to him, ducked under his swing to lightly tap him on the chest with the sparring stick.

"Goddess Above!" He took a step back, not ready for that kind of speed.

"I win." I pulled away from him, smiling.

Raven just groaned. "Cannot take you anywhere without you trying to fight someone."

"You were sparring them first," I pointed out.

"That is because we are closer to the same level than you and he are. It was more of a fair fight than this was." He threw the drying cloth at me. "Here, get dry before you get a chill, and Howling Wolf yells at me."

The lead warrior wobbled a little. "Did you say Howling Wolf?"

"Yes, she is his second, and I guess they would be partners, if City Elves could love," Raven explained as he handed me my thick leathers and daggers, then giving me my pelt.

The lead warrior stumbled back away from me. "You are partners with that vicious monster of an Elf?"

I looked to Raven, then back to the lead warrior. "He is only vicious when he needs to be, just like me. Why does that bother you?"

"He killed an entire Clan's warrior population."

"I know. He told me after I killed an entire troupe of slavers."

"You did not kill them, Snow. You slaughtered them. Use the correct terminology," Raven mumbled under his breath.

I ignored him. "He killed them because they killed the wife of our Elder. One of you would have done the same if something like that happened to your Clan. It is how he was chosen to be our Enforcer."

"Goddess Above, I am glad you two are here for peace instead of a war."

My eyes became blue as a warning. "We do not fight allies, but understand, if any of you had shown any inclination that Viper was not alone in his perversion, then I would have slaughtered whoever it was. As it stands, we are allies and as such, we will be there to help protect you if and when you need it. And through our alliance with the Star Clan, you would receive their help as well."

"Howling Wolf and Ursus?"

I smiled sweetly. "Yes."

"Do I even want to know how that happened?"

I shook my head, but Raven answered, "Snow thought it was a brilliant idea to answer a summons to a fight against Ursus, knowing that it was a fight to the death. She poisoned our Elder, Grandfather, Howling Wolf, and First Son, stole the letter from the Star Clan as proof she was from the Moon Clan. She then not only fought Ursus, but she also beat him, showed him mercy, then somehow convinced their Elder into an alliance."

The warriors stood there, staring at us, then they broke into hysterics. "Goddess Above, I am gladder that you came here for peace."

"You broke them." Bunny's voice drifted from near where Raven was standing.

The warriors all sobered up.

I turned and smiled at her. "Did you get to talk with your sister?"

"Yes, and again, thank you, Snow."

"Any time." I looked up at the sky, before going back to Raven. "We need to leave."

He looked up and saw the same cloud as I did. "Agreed."

Bunny handed me a pouch. "Here is something for you to take back to your Elder and Grandfather. I also added something in there for you, as a thank you for everything you have done for me."

I put the pouch into the pocket I had asked Xerinae to sew into my pelt. As I got close to her, I said, "You will heal. It will take time, but you are strong enough to not let what happened break you."

She nodded.

Raven grabbed my shoulder. "Come on, Snow, before we have to walk through your namesake." We waved to the Water warriors and Elder and headed back to the Moon Clan village. "Will she truly be alright?"

"She thinks she is weak because she could not stop what was happening," I said, "but I know that she will be able to overcome it one day. I told her how, and she has already started to heal a little. She was less shaky around the warriors than she was before."

He did not say anything until we came within sight of the village. "The Elder said that if we needed her warriors to liberate the City Elves, she is willing to send them."

I stopped. "She said what? But I told her that I was not even asking our own warriors to help."

"Apparently, our Elder and the Elder of the Star Clan have decided that when the time comes, we will fight for the City Elves' freedom. So, when the Water Clan Elder signed the document, she agreed to assist as well." He turned to look at me, and when he saw the tears on my cheeks, his eyes widened.

He whistled to the village, and Howling Wolf jogged over to us.

"What did you do to her?" he growled at Raven.

Raven put his hands up in submission. "I just told her that the Elders have decided that we would help the Matriarch and her with the City Elves. And on that note, I am going to leave before you snap at me." He ran away from the two Enforcers.

Howling Wolf swept me into his arms. "The Elder decided on it when he heard that the Star Clan warriors are willing to fight for your people's freedom. He made sure to let the Matriarch know before she left, so she could carry the alliance documents with her. She cried, too, and I think Lynx had the same reaction Raven did to it."

I sobbed into his shirt, warring emotions between relief, joy, and fear for my Clan's warriors getting hurt hit me all at once.

"Let me get you home, so you can warm by the fire while you let your emotions out." He carried me to our home, before he helped me out of my clothes, down to my linen top and bottoms.

He started to walk out to leave me to my emotions, but I stopped him and said, "Stay with me a little bit longer?"

He kissed my head. "I would love to, but it is about to snow, so I need to check on everyone first. Then, I will get us something to eat and come back." I went to get dressed, but he stopped me. "You stay here and get warm first. It should not take me more than ten minutes to check on everything Then, you can help warm me up." He kissed my cheek, before leaving our home.

I walked over to the bed and flopped on it. I grabbed my pillow and let my dam of emotions to erupt. I allowed myself to hope that everything would be all right, that none of those I cared about would get hurt, and that we would save all the City Elves. I allowed myself that hope, because reality would crush it the first chance it would get because even with the best laid plans, there are always casualties in a war.

Chapter 20

Ten Years Later

"That is another Clan who has agreed to help us," the Matriarch told me while we were updating the map of who all agreed to help. She bounced in excitement. "We have most of the Wood Elf Clans agreeing to help us, but it took entirely too long to get this far."

"It has only been ten years since we started this quest. That is quick when it comes to our lifespans," I replied. "We can only move so quickly without drawing the attention of the humans. I mean, we have been able to do raids on slave holding areas, but without getting the laws changed or stopping it at its source, there is only so much we can do."

"Matriarch!" One of the City Elf males came running into the room.

"Yes?"

"We received news that the humans have captured a Wood Elf Clan!"

She and I stiffened at the news before she sprang into action. "Go get Lynx to grab First Son and Howling Wolf, then send our Courier to the Star Clan to get Cristata and Ursus."

"Get Sparrow, too, and tell her to bring healing herbs."

"Yes, Matriarch, Enforcer!" He ran back out of the room.

"Goddess Above, they really did it. Those idiot humans really went after a Wood Elf Clan," she mumbled to herself, so I did not reply to her.

I looked at the map, then rolled it up. It would not take long for them to get to the settlement, so I wanted to be ready. "I will get the message and see where it came from."

"It should be at the Courier's office," she told me. "I will start gathering things we will need for this meeting. I have a feeling it is going to be a long night."

I left her to her duties, heading to the Courier's office.

The City Elf male behind the counter saw me and handed me the letter he received. He was maybe a couple inches taller than me, which made it easy to read his face.

"How bad?"

He shook his head. "It was bad, Enforcer. The Wood Elves who are a part of the slave trade waited until the males were gone and kidnapped all the women and children. When the males returned, the enemy burned the village to the ground. Not many of the warriors survived or escaped. The humans do not understand how the Wood Elves are different than we are. The Wood Elves do not know how vicious humans can be. We thought this day would come, but all of us hoped it would not."

I thanked him for the message. "We will get them back, along with the rest of our brethren."

A look passed between us, and I knew what he was thinking before he said, "But how many of them will be the same after the experience?"

I left him there, leaving both of us to our thoughts.

I went into the larger meeting room and opened the map. Then I read the letter and marked on the captured village and the Wood Elves responsible on the map. After the Water Clan sent my warning to their allies, those Clans forwarded the threat to other Clans, until there were only a couple of Clans who continued to dabble in the slave trade. It was not long until First Son, Howling Wolf, Sparrow, Cristata, and Ursus arrived, the Matriarch escorting them, holding food and drink for the long night.

I explained to them what the letter said and watched as they became angrier with each word I said.

"We have to go after them," Ursus growled.

I shook my head. "We need to get rid of the last two Clans who refuse to stop capturing slaves. If we do not stop those two, then they will continue to prey on the weaker Clans."

"You are talking about leaving Wood Elves in the hands of humans!" he roared.

"Yes." I stood up to him. "I do not like it either, but we have to stop more from being taken. I have seen your race and the resilience you all have." I let out a shaky breath. "But if more become enslaved, then we have other things to worry about."

Cristata touched Ursus on the arm before asking, "What do you mean?"

I looked at the Matriarch, both of us hoping to never have had to explain this.

She answered for me, "If more become enslaved, especially partners of warriors, then humans gain leverage over the Wood Elves they are fighting. Think of it this way, if you were captured and Ursus was told that the only way to keep you safe was to capture other Elves, what would he choose?"

The Wood Elves looked to each other.

"I do not know," she finally answered.

"There is a reason City Elves do not love. They used to be able to control us that way, but through the generations, we lost that ability as a way of self-preservation," I explained. "Next problem is that with more Wood Elves captured, the higher likelihood that they will be killed. Right now, Wood Elves would be the jewel in the crown of whoever owns them because they are still rare. If we do not stop the Clans who are working with the slavers, Wood Elf slaves would become more common, so they would be more likely to get killed if they rebel. Literally, the only thing that kept me alive for so long was because of how rare my silver hair is."

"What do you suggest?" First Son asked.

"First, we need to send messages to all the Clans we are allies with, explaining that if they are enslaved to not fight them. I know fighting is bred into you all, but it is imperative that none of the Wood Elves get hurt or killed," the Matriarch told them.

"Second, we will hunt down the slaver Clans and slaughter them. I already warned them what would happen if they chose to continue with the slave trade," I spoke next.

"Third, we will talk with our human ally family to make sure they spread the message that the Reckoning is coming, so the City Elves can prepare the newly enslaved Wood Elves," she continued.

I gave them a smile that sent shudders through them, "Finally, we go get our brethren. We stop the slave trade at the source."

Sparrow spoke softly. "You are talking about starting a war."

Howling Wolf kept his eyes on mine.

"No..." The Matriarch smiled.

I let them see the dead look in my eyes. Howling Wolf and First Son were the only ones who had seen it before. Sparrow, Cristata, and Ursus gasped as they understood.

"We are talking about ending one that they started the day they first captured City Elves, then escalated with the Wood Elves."

Howling Wolf took a shuddering breath in. "Then, let us get started." He used the map to help us plan out how he would suggest we go. "Ursus, First Son, Snow, and I will go to the village that was captured first. We will send them back here, where the Matriarch and Cristata can explain to them how we are going to get their families back, while they recover. Sparrow, we will need you here to help them heal. Then, the four of us will go to these two slaver Clans. If we find any captured Wood Elves, we will send them back down here. We will return, after you talk with your human ally family."

He continued, "Then, we gather up our allies and get them here to neutral ground. With our combined forces, we will leave some warriors to protect the settlement, while the rest of the warriors start our campaign to liberate the City Elves. Use your human ally family to tell us where they are located, and to warn the humans they trust to release the Elves in our care. We will send them back here with more warriors to make sure that our people are protected with the might of our alliance. Finally, we will take a small group to liberate the Elves who live in the Capital City."

I added, "While in the Capital City, I know where the City Elves will be held." I looked up to the Matriarch. "Do you trust your ally family with your life and the lives of your people?"

She nodded. "I do. Given the chance, they would abolish the slave trade completely."

"We better hope so. Because I have a feeling they will be the only ones who will stop a slaughter," I said.

"All right, let us get going, then," First Son told us, as he copied the map piece that we needed. "Keep Lynx here and send Couriers to our allies with the plan."

"Stay safe, my friends," the Matriarch said before we headed outside.

I gave Cristata and Ursus privacy, as well as First Son and Sparrow.

"Are you ready for this?" I asked Howling Wolf. "There is a chance we will not make it back alive. Especially, you and I since we will be the first on the field to fight."

"I am." He grabbed me and lifted me to meet his eyes, "I trust that the Goddess and Her Dark Consort will protect us. Moreover, you and I will be together, as we will be fighting at each other's sides. We are Enforcers, so there is no worthier death than to fight for those we wish to protect. There is no worthier life than to fight for what is right. Just promise me something."

"Anything," I said without hesitation.

"When we get back, will you become my partner officially and allow us to exchange our vows to spend the rest of our long lives together?"

"Are you sure? Then you will never get to choose a more feminine, gentle woman."

"For the past fifteen years, I knew that I wanted to spend the rest of my life with you, not with a woman who cannot throw me to the ground while we fight, despite how cute and tiny she is."

"If that is what you want, then yes. When we get back, I will marry you." I kissed him. "Until then, we have work to do."

He set me back on the ground.

Sparrow came over and gave a kit of healing herbs and bandages to First Son, Ursus, Howling Wolf, and myself. "You all better come back, or I will beat you black and blue." Her eyes were watery with tears that threatened to fall. "You take care of them, Silent Snow. You bring them home at all costs."

I hugged her. "I will. They are in good hands... and claws." I blinked, the Snow Cat rising from her den. I could feel how tired she was, so I made an internal vow that we would part ways after getting the City Elves free from slavery. She purred against my mind, accepting my offer. I turned to the forest and said, "Let us go."

Chapter 21

We arrived at the burned village a few days later. I grabbed my daggers and held them in my hands just in case we were attacked. "Hello?" I called out. "Is there anyone here?" silence filled the air, until I heard the thrum of the bow string being released. I used the Snow Cat's speed to block the arrow from hitting Ursus. I ran to the source of the arrow from and found two warriors who were ready to shoot again. "Are you Clansmen of the Sun Clan?"

"Why do you care, City Elf? Is it not enough that our families were taken because there were not enough vermin like you to buy and sell between the humans?" one of them said, his low voice tinged with pain.

"I care because we are here to save your families." I dropped next to him, as my allies came over to where we were. I used my dagger to tear his top, being careful near where his blood had clotted to his shirt. "He is hurt pretty badly."

First Son knelt next to me. "I will see what I can do."

I looked to the other male, who was shaking from exhaustion. "Here, drink slowly." I opened my waterskin and helped him drink it. "We are here from the Moon and Star Clans."

"Why would our enemies help us? Our Clan is no ally to either of yours," the injured male groaned.

"Because we are allies to anyone hurt by the slave trade. You are all Wood Elves, which transcends any petty thing that happened in the past," I told them.

Ursus explained further, "We received your letter from the Matriarch of the City Elf settlement about what happened."

The male who was drinking stopped. "We did not send a letter."

I whipped around, before an arrow buried next to the male I was talking with. "Ambush!" I yelled to my comrades. I watched as one of the slaver Clans came out of the forest. I recognized a few of them as being the ones who had kidnapped two of the Candidates during the Gauntlet. "You..."

Howling Wolf stood with me. "Ursus, you and First Son take care of these two. We have these bastards."

One of the three males who kidnapped the Candidates laughed. "Who knew that this village was under their alliance. It was a good idea to send that letter to that City Elf bitch." He then saw me. "I remember you." He moved his top to the side to show where the arrow had hit him in the shoulder. "I have been looking forward to this for almost fifteen years."

"If you want to kill me, get to the back of the queue." I stood there ready for them.

"Kill the Wood Elves, leave the bitch to me," he told his people.

I smiled to Howling Wolf. "See you on the other side."

He nodded, giving me permission.

I rushed forward, before the leader could react. I plunged my knife into his chest, between two ribs, before slashing him across the throat. The other slavers stared as I ripped my knife from his chest, until Howling Wolf came for them. I followed his lead, our deadly dance as the two of us moved through their ranks. It did not take long until we killed the last of them.

Howling Wolf caught my arm at the end. "You are getting faster, even without the Snow Cat."

I walked him back over to where the other males were. "She wants release, so I promised that after we saved the other Elves, that I would let her continue to the Underworld."

He went off to grab something that caught his eye.

First Son looked up at me. "Have a little bit of fun there?"

I smiled. "You know it. Killing slavers brings joy to my cold, dead heart." I looked at the two fallen Wood Elves. "Will they survive long enough to get back to Sparrow?"

"We will try. Ursus and I will take them since it is obvious you two will not need us for the slaver Clans. We will meet you two back at the settlement," First Son said.

I took out the kit that Sparrow gave me. "Here, you will need more since you will not be able to move as fast with them injured as they are."

He took it from me. "Stay safe, you two."

"Do not have too much fun without us." Ursus grinned.

"This should help a little bit." Howling Wolf came back with a slaver horse and its covered cage. "I know that it looks bad, but since time is of the essence, it will have to do."

I held the horse while they loaded the two fallen Wood Elves into the cage, keeping the door open. "Is there anyone else in your Clan here?"

The less injured male shook his head. "No, they are either dead, or they were captured."

"We will get your Clans mates back," I promised them.

"Thank you, City Elf," the more injured male said.

"Just get healed up, so you can be ready." I smiled at them, before lowering the blanket so they could get some rest. I walked up to Ursus. "Keep your axe ready, just in case you need to fight. Also, keep your alliance document handy, in case other allies question a slave cage going through their territories."

"Will do. Stay safe, Snow, Wolf." He waved to us then snapped the reins to get the horse moving.

I looked to Howling Wolf. "I hope we get there before they get sold..."

"Same," he answered as we went through the forest to find the village of this slaver Clan. We found it, but there was no one there. We wandered through the village, ready for an ambush. "What is going on?"

"I do not know..." I thought about it. "Howling Wolf, how many males do you think were at the burned village? Like enough to be all warriors?"

He thought about it, understanding crossing his face. "They did not..."

We searched through the entire village, not finding anyone.

"Is there anyone here?" I called out.

I heard a child's cry, which brought out the Snow Cat. "Wait!"

Howling Wolf tried to stop me, but the Snow Cat snarled at him.

"Let me come with you, so do not take off at full speed without me." He let me go, and I ran to where the child was crying. The little boy must have been only six hundred years old, but more than half my height.

I kept my ear pricked for any more noises, while Howling Wolf checked on the boy. When the bigger Wood Elf got close, the boy screamed in terror, so I ripped him away from the child. The child ran and cling to me. I let the Snow Cat comfort him with her purrs, using my voice. Every time the child saw Howling Wolf, he screamed, so the older Wood Elf went to check other buildings.

"What happened, Kitten?" I carried him outside into the open air, sitting him in my lap, while I rocked him.

"The warriors..." He sniffled. "Sold our Clan!" He yelled as he started to cry again.

I rubbed his hair. "It is all right, Kitten. Did three of the warriors have arrow wound scars in their shoulders?"

"Yes, they were our top warriors, and one was my father. They killed the Elder and took Grandmother." He sniffled again, a sob almost escaping. "They took our Clan and sold them with the other Clan they stole. They kept talking about riches while the humans took our Clan away."

I kept rocking him. "It is all right, Kitten. We will get your Clan back safely. Were the warriors the only ones who wanted to take part in selling Elves to the humans?"

He nodded into my shoulder. "Elder did not like them selling Elves at all. They did it behind Elder's back."

I saw Howling Wolf watching, but he shook his head. I pulled the boy away a little. "This is my friend, Wolf. He is going to help us stand back up, and he will make sure that your Clan is safe, all right, Kitten?"

He turned to see Howling Wolf standing there. The boy shook.

"Be brave, Kitten. He is our friend, so he will make sure we do not get hurt."

Howling Wolf took slow steps to us, before going behind me to pick me and the boy up to stand.

"See? He is a gentle Forest God."

The boy looked at Howling Wolf in wonder. "Forest God?"

285

I smiled at him. "Exactly, you see, Wolf here had the power of protection around him. Just as the Forest protects Her creatures, he will protect you and me." Howling Wolf looked embarrassed because he always blushed when I called him a Forest God. "My name is Snow. Do Kittens have names?"

The boy shook his head. "Not until I am older."

"What is your mother's name?"

"Resting Doe. She is a very pretty lady, and she tells me I look like her first partner before he died," he said.

Howling Wolf straightened up more, rage covering his face. I put the boy's face to my shoulder. "Leash your anger, Enforcer." I used my other hand to tell him. "Then you shall be my Kitten until we find your Clan."

"Why Kitten?" he asked, letting his mind get away from the horrors he dealt with in his short life.

"I have a Snow Cat spirit inside of me, and she had Kittens that she could not protect before she passed away. She wants you to be safe, so as her Kitten, she will protect you with her life. And I believe that everyone should be able to be called something."

"Can we leave here, Snow?" he asked.

"Of course. Do you mind if Wolf holds you for a little bit? I just need to make sure of something."

He nodded into my shoulder.

"Such strong and brave, Little Kitten." I told him, as Howling Wolf lifted him from my arms. I shook my arms out. "How about you ask him why his name is Wolf?"

I left them to check through the buildings until I found the book I was looking for. All Sellers had a ledger, where they track who was bought and sold. For City Elves, it would list our brands, but for the unbranded Wood Elves, it might have names. I took it with me, going back to Howling Wolf and the Kitten.

"I knew your mother a long time ago," Howling Wolf was telling the boy.

"You did?" His eyes seemed to light up.

"She came from my Clan, where she was a healer. She met a warrior in the woods, and they fell in love. She decided that her love for him was worth more to her than her Clan, so she joined his," he explained, before he saw me. There was war of emotions on his face, until he blanked his eyes to me.

I signed to him with my hands that this was not the time or place.

He struggled to regain his composure. He turned the boy to face me. "Snow says we are ready."

"Howling Wolf is going to take you somewhere safe, Kitten. I have to go get a book from another Clan nearby." Howling Wolf scowled as he realized that I was planning on going alone. He started to argue, but I stopped him. "I am just going to forest walk to get the book, nothing else, Howling Wolf." I smiled at him innocently, and I knew that he knew I was lying.

I walked over and kissed the boy on the head. "Keep being brave, Kitten. Howling Wolf is going to take you to our Clan, so that his sister, Sparrow, can make sure everything is alright. There is a lady in our Clan named Xerinae who makes the best food in the whole world, so make sure you eat something. I will be there soon. I promise."

"Stay safe, Snow." The boy smiled.

Howling Wolf looked like he wanted to say something but chose not to. "Be careful, Snow. Happy hunting."

I nodded, not trusting my voice. I then ran out of the village, using the Snow Cat's speed and vision to guide my steps. I tried not to think about the rage I saw on Howling Wolf's face, or the warring emotions in his eyes. I kept trying to stop hearing the love in his voice when he talked about Doe. I knew that he would have chosen someone like her over me, so why did I believe him when he said he wanted me?

"Because Doe was no longer in his life. But she will be as soon as we rescue her and her Clan," I told myself, hating the dead sound of my voice.

I reached the second slaver Clan sometime later, unhindered by the Wood Elves who were normally with me. I drew my daggers and stepped into the village.

"Come out and play, you slaver cowards!" I yelled to them.

This village reminded me of the human one we found the Matriarch in, all males with few females, though they were chained. I wanted to let my daggers taste the blood of this Clan.

"It is a City Elf!"

"She is wearing clothes of the Enforcer of the Moon Clan."

"Look at her hair! It must be 13-87-22! She will make us rich!"

"Does she really think she can beat all of us with two little knives?"

The slavers murmurs broke the silence of the forest.

The women slaves retreated inside, leaving only the slavers and me.

Their Elder came out with their Grandmother, a hard woman who looked like she was ready to kill me as well.

"Get her!" the Elder shouted, and they surrounded me.

I let the Snow Cat take my pain and rage and turn it into a rain of blood and death. I gracefully moved through them, killing them as I went. I hated them because they were the ones who bought and sold my people. I ignored the pain from their attacks, just as Howling Wolf taught me. Soon, it was down to the Elder, Grandmother, and me. I wanted to carve the Elder to pieces, but I needed to get the ledger.

"Give me your ledger, and I will kill you quickly instead of the slow bleed out like you deserve."

The Elder took off the boar pelt he wore and grabbed a large, metal whip from his hip. "You will pay for this, slave."

"Then come and punish me."

He cracked the metal whip, the sound of chains combining with the smell of metal blood brought forth memories from my slavery. I did not see the Elder standing there; instead, I saw a myriad of masters, holding a whip covered in my and other slave's blood.

I growled, much deeper than my voice should have been able to go.

He took a step forward, lashing my arm with the tip of the metal whip.

I caught the metal whip, using my dagger to hold it close to my arm.

He was stronger than me, so he was able to easily rip it away from me, slashing my arm as it pulled away from me.

I let the Snow Cat take over completely. Her moves forced my body forward. She danced around the Elder's whip, not getting hit with it again. He changed the momentum of the whip at the last second, wrapping around my arm. I kicked my foot up, catching the whip under my instep, pulling it to the ground. I threw the whip off my arm, then launched myself forward. The Snow Cat let me take back over as I stabbed him in the stomach, spun around, and ripped him apart like I did Viper. Blood and ticker things clung to my skin and clothes.

He dropped to the ground, as I walked over to the Grandmother. "Ledger or you will follow him to the Underworld."

Terror filled in her eyes as she stared at me. She pulled it from the inside of her top. She tossed it to me, before she threw the knife that was hiding in her top at me.

I was too focused on the ledger to dodge the knife. I caught it in the shoulder, a hot searing pain spreading through me. I ripped it out of my shoulder and used my dominant hand to slam her dagger into her throat.

She gargled blood as she fell.

The searing heat became worse, and I knew that she had poisoned it with something. I fell to my knees.

A beautiful Wood Elf slave came from where she had been hiding. She shouted to another slave, "Get the antitoxin!" She caught me as I fell face first into the ground. "Hold on, City Elf." Her voice was warm and friendly.

"You must be Doe..." Her silky black hair fell in waves around her, accenting her dark brown eyes and skin.

She looked surprised. "I am."

I closed my eyes, trying to fight off the pain to tell her, "Howling Wolf has your Kitten. He is safe..." That was as far as I could get before, I passed out from the pain and poison.

Chapter 22

There were sheets and a soft bed under me. "Where?"

"Sh. You are still very weak from that poison the Grandmother had in her dagger," the same warm voice from before told me. "How do you know Howling Wolf? And you found my son?"

"Starting with a less painful answer, yes, we found your son. Howling Wolf took him back to the Moon Clan. As for Howling Wolf himself, I am his Second."

"I can see why you would be, after seeing you decimate the slaver Clan here." She looked at me, eyes wide. "How did you become a part of the Moon Clan? They are usually very wary of strangers."

"Escaped slavery, attacked Howling Wolf for his wolf pelt, killed a bear, earned a name, saved First Son's life, then became Enforcer after killing a group of slavers and passing the test. Working with the Matriarch to save City Elves..." My eyes widened, as I struggled to get up, "Have to go!"

"Oh no, you do not. You need to rest some more." She held me down.

"Cannot. Matriarch cannot do it on her own." I teared up from the pain and weakness and worry. "Clans are going to City Elf settlement, so I need to be there before the warriors leave towards the Capital City."

"You have to at least wait until the other women get the wagon ready. They can survive without you for a couple of days. You do not want Howling Wolf mad at you for not healing correctly, right?"

"I do not care what he gets mad about."

She jumped back, confused.

I used that time to sit up.

"You are his Second."

"Does not mean anything beyond working with him. He still loves you, so there is no point in lying in saying that there is something between him and I."

She covered her mouth with her hand. "Even after all of this time? He still loves me?" The tears shimmered in her eyes, which just made me want to get away from her even faster. She turned back into the Healer when I tried to get out of the bed. "Goddess Above, just stop before you tear the stitches."

"That is fine. It will just add more scars."

"Will you stop?" she pleaded.

"No," I told her as I grabbed my top, sniffing it. The blood and gore had been washed away. I put it on and winced. "Where are my daggers and sheaths?"

"Goddess Above, you have to be an Enforcer if you care more about those things than your own body." She picked them up, then noticed the embroidery on them. "What are these for?"

"Because I am his Second, his sister thought it would be hilarious to embroider them that way," I lied, pushing down the betrayal I felt from the sheaths. I then grabbed the side of the bed and took off the sheets and blanket. I swung my legs over the side and took a deep breath. Testing the strength of one leg, then the other, I tried to stand. "If you want to see your son, I suggest we head out sooner rather than later." I grabbed my pants and carefully dressed. She handed me my daggers. I realized my arms were covered in bandages, but I did not care.

She sighed, deciding that trying to stop me was useless. She came around to where I was and helped me walk to where the other women were almost ready to leave in the covered cage. She tried to get me into the back, but I refused, never wanting to be in the back of one of these wagons ever again.

"Suit yourself, Enforcer," she growled, as she grabbed some things before everyone was ready. They climbed into the wagon and one of the women snapped the reins.

I led her toward the City Elf settlement, praying that I would not be too late to leave. It took a week to get there, but when we arrived, First Son was there to greet us.

"Snow!" He reached for me at the seat of the wagon. "What happened? Where is Howling Wolf?"

"He should have beaten me back. We found Doe's son in one of the Slaver Clans."

Sparrow noticed my injuries "Get Snow to the Matriarch to debrief." She then asked me, "Did you say Doe's son?"

"Yes?" Doe came out of the back of the wagon, and First Son dropped me on accident.

"Really?" I growled at him from the ground.

"Goddess Above, First Son! Do not drop her!" Sparrow came over and grabbed me. She glared at Doe, then turned to me. "What do you mean he should have been here first?"

"We found Doe's kitten, and we parted ways, while I took care of the other Slaver Clan to get their ledger." I handed both books to First Son. "It has every slave purchased and sold. The

Matriarch can use them to track how many City and Wood Elves are enslaved."

"Do you think--?" Sparrow started, but I stopped that thought.

"No, he would have fought and never would have been captured."

"Except he had Doe's son..." First Son looked between Doe and me. "If they threatened the child..."

I felt my world collapse under me. "I am going after him."

"No, you are not," the Elder spoke as he stepped out of the Matriarch's building. "We have a plan, and you need to stick to it."

"Honorable Elder." Doe bowed to him gracefully.

"It has been too long, Resting Doe," the Elder told her. "I want a full report of what happened."

"Yes, Elder." She turned to me. "She was stabbed in the shoulder with a knife."

"I am fine," I tried to tell them, until Sparrow touched the spot, and I winced in pain. "I will be fine," I amended.

"You better be, Silent Snow," the Matriarch growled. "Because if you are not, I will beat you black and blue." She looked to the Elder. "We will give Howling Wolf a couple more days, before we start the next part of the plan. If he is not here by then, I will get into contact with my human ally family to see what they know. Until then, sit on her if you must, but she needs to be healed by then."

"Raven! Help Sparrow with Silent Snow," the Elder called over to where our other warriors were. "Resting Doe, come with First Son, the Matriarch, and I."

Raven and Sparrow helped me get into the bathhouse. She stripped me to check the stab wound. "Goddess Above, Snow!" She undid all the bandages and saw the extent of the damage. "What caused these?"

"Metal whip," I told her. "Sparrow?" I felt my emotions wrecking through me.

"Yes, Snow?"

"I found Doe... Her partner is dead, and I killed the male she was currently with."

"You must have had a good reason."

"Her new partner was one of the Slavers who attacked us during the Gauntlet. Her son says that she says he looks like her first partner." I felt tears spill out. "He still loves her. I saw it in his face and eyes when he was talking to the Kitten."

Sparrow hugged me. "I am sorry, Snow. You do not deserve this."

"I promised him that I would step aside if he wanted a delicate flower, so I will. But why does it hurt so badly?"

"It is called a heart break, Snow," Raven explained. "I know City Elves do not usually know love, but I believe you may have stumbled on it by being with us for the past fifteen years."

"I want it to go away," I told them.

"It does not work like that, Snow," Sparrow said. "But we can fix up these wounds to get you ready to fight." She and Raven worked together to check on the new scabs that covered me from my fight with the slaver Clans. She then checked on the stab wound, and I heard her suck in a sharp breath. "Goddess Above." She began to work on it. "How did you get stabbed like this?"

"Grandmother of Slaver Clan threw a knife after she gave me their ledger."

"As much as I hate to say it, I am glad Doe was there to help you."

"How is she doing?" The Matriarch came into the bathhouse and stared at the wound. "Oh Goddess."

"It does not feel as bad as it looks."

"That is because you are feeling emotional pain, and that tends to override your physical pain," Raven told me. "I have seen you do this before, especially when riding some sort of emotional problem."

"Doe told us everything that happened on her side. She was partnered with the warrior from that other Clan, but he was killed after a raid of Slaver warriors hit their village. From then on, she was forced to be with one of the Slaver warriors, as were the other women. Their Elder was killed after the warriors attempted to enslave that other Wood Elf village. She was sold with the other women of her Clan to the village where you found her. She was surprised that Howling Wolf had a Second."

"That is all I am, Matriarch. He still loves her, so there is no point in fighting it."

"Not so fast, Snow." The Matriarch looked down at me. "Are you really going to give up on him that easily?"

"I told him years ago that I would step aside if he wanted another woman. He and I are not official, and now that Doe is back in the picture, there is no denying it." I tried to sound nonchalant, but she knew better.

"If you wanted someone new, you could have broken it off. You do not need to come up with this narrative to do it," she said plainly.

"You did not see his face or his eyes!" I yelled at her, giving an outlet to my anger. "You did not see the rage on his face when he learned her partner was dead! You did see the warring emotions of him still loving her, then looking at me and seeing regret! You did not see the hope on his face when he talked to the Kitten! You. Were. Not. There. Matriarch!" My voice echoed in the bathhouse.

"I may not have been, but I have seen you two enough that I know better." She bent down to my level. "When he gets here, we will see what happens. If he chooses her, I will do a Test of Taking against him. If he truly wants her, then I will tell your Elder that you belong to my settlement as my Enforcer, so it will not be thrown in your face every day. But if he chooses you... Do you want to spend the rest of your life with your Forest God of an Enforcer?"

I pushed myself up. "He will not choose me. Not when it is between her and I." I wobbled a little but used my stubbornness to keep upright. "I am going to lie down. In two days, whether he is here or not, I am going to your human ally's home and will request that they take me to a slave auction in the Capital City. I will stop the slavery at the source, while the Clans continue to follow the original plan," I told them, then escaped to find my way to a tree at the edge of the village.

"Snow?" a familiar male voice spoke.

"Not in the mood, First Son," I said without looking back at him.

"I just wanted to say that I am worried, too," he told me, then he helped me into the tree, climbing up after me. "He should have been here by now, and it is not like him to be late like this, especially because of how important it is to stick together."

"I chose to leave, because I saw the look he had when he found out that Doe had a son that we rescued." I sighed. "After I saw the look of hope in his eyes, I decided to go on my own to the other Slaver Clan's village. I needed to burn off rage, so I went there and slaughtered them. We were supposed to stay together, but I gave him the son to watch, so I would not have to see him pining over her."

"It will be all right, Snow. If he has been captured, we will get him back. If he shows up here, I will let you throw him into the dirt for making us worry." He tried to cheer me up, and it helped. "Are you planning on being here for the night?"

"Yes, I just need some time to myself for a bit."

"I will bring you food after it is made. The other Clans arrived a couple of days ago, so Xerinae has been cooking up a storm."

"How were the males you and Ursus brought back?"

"They will live, but I doubt they will be well enough to fight, so we are going to leave them here to help protect the settlement."

"Good night, First Son." I leaned back against the trunk of the tree.

"Good night, Snow," he replied and climbed down.

I yawned and let the healing sleep take over me.

Chapter 23

"Howling Wolf still is not here." Sparrow sounded beyond concerned the night I woke up from my healing sleep, my shoulder no longer in pain.

"Well, tomorrow, we start liberating Elves, so if he was captured, we will find him." First Son held her hand.

Xerinae plopped some food down in front of them, while I helped her disperse some to the rest of the gathered Clans. She passed by me. "Are you doing all right, Snow?"

I shrugged, as I set food down in front of Ursus and Cristata. None of them questioned why I chose not to speak, giving into the silence I spent most of my life in.

Once everyone had their food, the Matriarch stood in front of the hundreds of gathered Wood Elves and her City Elves.

"I would like to thank everyone for being here. Words cannot explain how grateful I am that you all decided to help our plight. With the addition of Wood Elves being taken, this is no longer a liberation of City Elves. Instead, our goal is to get all our brethren out from the disgusting practice of slavery. Tonight, we gather our strength and tomorrow, Silent Snow and others from the Moon Clan will lead our warriors to release the Elven slaves."

"With each place they pass, warriors will escort our brothers and sisters here. Then, Silent Snow and a smaller group of warriors will head to the Capital City to get those trapped there. We have a human ally family who has agreed to help us, in exchange for letting their family live. After talking with the Elders, if this family does as requested, we have decided that they will become our human liaisons, meaning they would fall under the protection of our alliance." She grabbed me. "Silent Snow will be playing the part of a myth that every City Elf knows. If any City Elf is terrified of you, tell them that you are with the Reckoning. They will understand that you are there to save them."

"Why would that help?" someone from the Water Clan asked.

"Pain and fear are very good ways to keep someone compliant. Many of you have seen Silent Snow's scars. Every City Elf has some, though not as bad." She pointed to Ursus. "Ursus of the Star Clan asked to feel why City Elves would not fight. Ursus, tell them what you felt, and if you would keep trying to fight after that."

Ursus shuddered before he stood up. "The Matriarch told me that it was the most painful thing I would ever feel, and she was correct. I was only lashed three times, but the pain exploded like fire over my body. I have had broken bones, been stabbed, slashed, almost killed, and nothing compared to the pain I felt from the lashing. Even I would never try to fight if that was a guarantee every time I rebelled." He looked to me and added, "The fact that Snow is covered in those scars is a testament of her inner strength. Do not believe that all City Elves or even our newly captured brethren would be willing to take those punishments if they have the choice."

"By using our mythical protector's name, you are more likely to get the City Elves to assist you instead of being fearful of you. We have been told for our entire captivity that Wood Elves would not only be worse than the humans, but they were also more likely to kill us. We need them to trust you for this to work."

"What is the myth that she is playing?" another Wood Elf asked her.

"How many of you know why Silent Snow is going to be leading this task?" she asked the Wood Elves.

Only those from the Moon Clan, the Star Clan, and Bunny raised their hands.

"Grandfather, may I request your assistance to show them her memory?"

"Only if Bunny is all right with it," I told her, looking at the younger woman.

She gave me a nod, a new strength of fire glinting in her soul. I held my hand out to Grandfather, so he could use my blood for his smoke memory magic. He took his blood and tossed it into the fire. I thought of when I killed Viper and focused on hearing the Matriarch's voice. I watched their faces as they saw me eviscerate Viper, while hearing the Matriarch's lyrical voice about the Reckoning. I would have been lying if I did not take pleasure in seeing Doe's distressed face. Seeing me kill someone was bad but seeing it from my point of view was worse.

"That is the part she is playing and why."

"I am glad we never took her on in battle."

"Thank the Goddess Above that we are on the same side."

"Can you imagine if the humans used her for their slave trade against us?"

"She could lead the charge, and I would gladly follow her into battle."

An older male chuckled. "Can you imagine being her partner, and she getting angry at you? Nowhere would be safe."

A small smile played on my lips at that comment.

"That is why we are using her as our myth. If you saw her kill and heard that she was the Goddess's protector, would you want to believe it is true?" The Matriarch smiled, before turning to me. "Thank you for showing them, Silent Snow."

"At your service, Matriarch." I gave her a quick bow, then sat next to First Son, Sparrow, Xerinae, Raven, and Lynx, leaving a spot next to Lynx for the Matriarch when she was done grandstanding.

She gave them all another thank you, promising that the warriors would leave at dawn. She sat down next to me. "We will get your Howling Wolf back, Snow." She patted me on the arm.

"I already told you that he is not mine," I told her before biting into my food.

"You do not really believe that." She sounded more concerned than shocked.

"Matriarch, we both know that I could never give him the love that Wood Elves want from their partners. Add in that compared to her, I am nothing beyond my ability able to fight and kill. If he was captured, I will find him and bring him home to her as she is his one true love. Now, I am asking as a friend for you to leave it alone."

"I have one last thing to say before I drop it. I swear to the Goddess Above and Her Dark Consort that if you do anything beyond your normal brand of stupidity because of these emotions, I will make sure that you regret it. Do you understand, Enforcer?"

"Yes, Matriarch." I sighed and then I continued to eat. I just wanted to go back to the tree already.

"Good." She turned to Sparrow and Raven and started to discuss what the warriors would need for healing supplies.

I finished eating, bid them a good night and went toward the tree I had been sleeping in.

"Silent Snow?" I winced as Grandfather called me over to where he, the other Grandfathers and Mothers, and Elders were eating.

"Yes, Grandfather?"

"Something is wrong, Grandchild?"

I knew better than to lie, but I also did not feel comfortable telling all of them about my heart problems. I signed about everything I saw and heard about Doe from Howling Wolf, and how I knew they still loved each other.

"You truly believe that he would choose her?" the Elder asked.

I nodded.

"Will you be well for tomorrow?"

I nodded again.

"I will do my job as the Enforcer, Honorable Elder. I will bring home as many of our warriors as I can, since the alliance falls under my purview, therefore under my protection."

"Thank you for speaking with me. Have a good night, Enforcer."

I bowed to the table. "Good night, Honorable Elders, Grandfathers, Grandmothers." I went to the tree and climbed up it easily. When I looked to where the Clans were talking, laughing, and preparing. Doe talked with the other women of her old and new Clans. Despite the worry she felt for her son, her face lit up like the brilliance of the sun. I turned away from them all and let myself fall asleep.

Chapter 24

Dawn came too early, but I was already awake. I cleaned myself in the bathhouse, pulling my hair back into a long braid, having neglected cutting it. I sharpened my daggers and put them into my embroidered sheaths. I felt more like the Reckoning as I put in my thick leathers over my black linen clothes.

Sparrow came into the bathhouse. "Snow?"

"Yes?"

She came running up and hugged me. "Promise me that you will stay safe and that you will bring them home."

"I promise." I hugged her back.

She whispered, "And if my idiot brother decides that he wants the bitch that left him, then I will beat him black and blue."

I laughed at that. "I will hold him for you. You stay safe here. We do not know how the humans are going to react to our attacks, so keep alert. It is one of the reasons why we are sending warriors back with the slaves, because there is no idea if they will attack this settlement with each success."

"I will, and you will always be my sister, Snow, even if my brother is too stupid to see how much better you are for him."

"All I ever wanted was freedom and a family. You and Howling Wolf gave me both. I will pay that kindness back." I gave her another quick hug when I heard the whistle calling the warriors. Then I ran outside to stand next to First Son. "Everyone ready?"

He looked back. "Ready as we ever will be."

The Matriarch handed both of us a map. "These are where the ledgers say the slaves have been sold to. I marked our human ally family as well. See them before you storm the Capital City, because they should be able to help you get in without being noticed." She hugged me. "Bring them home, Enforcer."

"I will, Matriarch. Keep everyone safe here, or there will be no home to return to. And if any human decides that now is a good time to attack, I believe the City Elves here will be able to show them the error of their ways."

She looked to the rest of the gathered warriors. "Yesterday, we were different races and Clans. Today, we are one. Come home where you belong and bring back your new brothers and sisters. Let the Goddess Above guide you, and may Her Dark Consort welcome your enemies to the Underworld!"

There was a roar of agreement behind us.

Her eyes fluttered with justice and fire. "Show them no mercy, Reckoning."

Chapter 25

We followed the maps, splitting our forces between First Son and me. We planned to meet at the human ally family's home; the Matriarch sent word to them to expect us. We reached many of the places where the City Elves were held. Upon seeing me, many of them fought against their captors. We gave the humans a choice, surrender their slaves or perish. Many chose to give their slaves up, but many also chose to fight and die. The warriors split off as planned, getting the City Elves back to the settlement.

Word spread throughout the kingdom of the Wood Elves coming to claim the City Elves. Some families decided that releasing their slaves before we reached them was a good plan. Others tasted my hatred as they killed my brethren before we could get to them. Blood had soaked the ground of the kingdom as we moved.

After a year of liberating the City Elves, we reached the human ally family, with their head of the household, Roland. First Son arrived the day before I did. Both of our warrior teams were down to a few. They gave their Elves up to us, happy that we were putting a stop to this barbaric practice.

Tiny feet came running to me.

"Snow!"

I caught the boy in my arms and hugged him. "Kitten! Have they been taking good care of you?"

"Yes! They kept the bad humans away from us!" He buried his face in my shoulder.

First Son looked at me, confused.

I pulled away. "Kitten, this is First Son. He is the son of our Elder and is Wolf's best friend. First Son, this is Doe's son."

"Nice to meet you." First Son's voice fell flat.

"Come on, Kitten. I have more friends I want you to meet, while I talk with Lord Roland and First Son." I brought him to Ursus, and the boy cowered a little. "This is Ursus, and he is one of my friends. He carries a big axe! How strong do you think you have to be to carry one as well? And look at this!" I pointed to his muscles. "I bet you could beat him, Kitten. Think you can throw him into the dirt?"

"Yes!" He sounded excited.

I set him down. "Do not go easy on him, Kitten." I kissed the top of the boy's head, then left him to spar with Ursus. I went inside the small manor house, where Roland was sitting with First Son.

Roland explained how the boy came to them. "He and another Wood Elf were on the auction block, but we had to make the choice, because we did not have the gold for both. We were unable to stop them from being branded, since they were branded upon capture. We decided to save the boy because he would have been raised as a pet, whereas the warrior could at least fend for himself. At least, I hope he could."

"You did the right thing. Can you imagine if he was used that way?" I told the older human male.

"What is a pet?" First Son asked me.

Roland looked uncomfortable answering, but I did not have that problem. "A pet is another name for a sex slave. At his age, he would most likely just be groomed for serving the bed, but there are those who enjoy younger flesh."

He paled. "What kinds of monsters do that to children?"

"Those who do not care that they are children," Roland answered. "Thank the Goddess that those monsters are few and far between, but even one is too many."

"What about the other Wood Elf?" I sipped on the tea.

"He was purchased by the royal family for their Queen's pleasure."

"May I inquire why you are trying to help us?" First Son asked.

"My family has been against it from the start, but the only way we could make sure they were not mistreated was to buy them ourselves. Human law forbids releasing slaves, so we chose to do what we could." He sighed, holding his mug of tea. "But we cannot keep up with the supply, especially since Wood Elves have been added. We know the Goddess would never want for Her children to be enslaved as they are. But we are only one family..."

I smiled at him. "You are doing everything you can to help. The Matriarch called you an ally because we heard stories of a family that was trying to help the City Elves, even if they had to buy us. We never heard anything about your family of any misdeeds. That means you are under our alliance and the protections we provide."

"Thank you." He then changed the subject and asked, "What is your plan to get into the Capital City?"

"I would say in disguise, but I am too short, and he is too tall."

Ursus came running in, holding the boy in his arms. "A Courier dropped this off." He handed Roland the message.

"Oh, Goddess Above!" the human male shouted, standing up. "I have to go!"

I grabbed the message, skimmed it, then raced after him. "Wait!" I stopped him as he mounted his horse. "It is a trap!"

"Does it matter? They will kill my children if I do not surrender!"

My brain whirled, as First Son and Ursus came running outside. The other warriors gathered around to see what the problem was.

"Trade me," I told the human.

"What?"

"Trade me for their lives."

"I cannot ask you to do that."

I looked to Ursus. "Get the Kitten home with the rest of the warriors."

First Son grabbed the message and read it. "Are you planning—"

"Yes, I am," I told him without hesitation. "It says they will use his children for Necromancy to stop the City Elf Rebellion that started in the Capital City. His family is under our protection, as such, I will protect them as I would do any other ally. We both know that they will not release your family unless you give them something worth more than their lives."

"And you are worth more?" Ursus asked me.

"Yes, not just because of my hair anymore. The City Elves are rebelling because they believe in the Reckoning. They believe in it because the Matriarch spread the rumor that I was the Goddess's protector. I may not have risen like wildfire, but I will be the reaper at the enemy's door to help them pay for their sins in blood."

"That is insane, Snow," First Son whispered.

"If it helps, this does fall under my normal stupidity, so both Sparrow and the Matriarch cannot get mad at me for it." I looked back to Roland and added, "This is the best move we can take, so let me help you."

He looked grateful but worried for his family. "Are you sure?"

I grinned. "What are a few more scars between friends? Just be ready to get your family out."

He nodded. "All right, if we are going to do this, we are going to do it right." He turned to Ursus and First Son. "Get your people out of here. They should not have to watch this, nor should they get involved."

First Son faced Ursus and said, "Take them back to the settlement. I am counting on you to keep everyone safe if this does not work how she hopes."

"Snow?" the boy asked me.

I reached up and touched his face. "It is all right, Kitten. Your mother is safe. Ursus will make sure that you see her as soon as you get back. Can you do me a huge favor and give Auntie Sparrow the biggest hug for me?"

He nodded.

"And you know what a Matriarch is, right?"

He nodded again.

"I need you to find her and punch her in the arm."

He beamed. "I will."

I looked to the other warriors and stated, "All of you are the greatest warriors I have ever met, and it was an honor to fight beside you this last year. You will need to return to the settlement, because if this does not go right, the humans will attack where they know us to be. I will either see you all again in this world, or in the Underworld after you all live long lives." I turned to First Son and said, "Last chance to choose to go home to Sparrow."

"If I leave you here, she will beat me black and blue." He looked to the warriors and commanded, "Get going."

We did not wait for them to leave as Roland hopped off his horse. "Let us hurry." He took us back into his home, where I stripped out of my clothes and into the plain dress worn by most female slaves.

First Son kept my daggers but placed one of his smaller knives into my boot. "You will get your daggers back when I get that knife back."

"What? You mean I cannot keep it? What kind of a gift is that?" I teased, trying to throw down the anxiety I was feeling about being back in slave attire.

Roland stared at my scars. "Goddess Above."

"Do you have a whip?" I asked him. "Because I doubt they would buy that I was captured without incident."

He shook his head. "I do not have one."

I looked to First Son. "Make it look good. And while I take care of Roland's family and help the royalty to the underworld, get the rest of the City Elves out."

"I will, and I am sorry, Snow," he apologized as he knocked me out, so I would not feel the pain of the beating he would give me.

Chapter 26

"It is a Wood Elf with Lord Roland!"

"What is he carrying?"

"Is that a silver haired City Elf?"

"Is she the one who caused the City Elf Rebellion?"

I woke up, draped over First Son's shoulder. I felt the bruises, but at least he did them in places where they would not hamper me in a fight. The familiar sounds of the Capital City drifted around me, despite not being here since I helped the Queen bleed to death after childbirth a couple centuries ago. A blindfold covered my eyes and shackles laid on my wrists. We entered an area where the shadows cooled the stones around us.

"What is the meaning of this, Lord Roland?" The male voice echoed off the walls.

First Son dropped me in front of him, and I sprawled to the ground. "We have brought you the 13-87-22, the City Elf who is known as the Reckoning by her people," Roland told them. "We bring her in exchange for my family, since she is worth more than they are combined."

"Guards, seize her and bring her here!" the voice yelled.

I tried to fight them off but being blindfolded made it harder.

Two guards grabbed my arms, and I was unable to pull away from them. They dragged me up to the location of the booming voice. He ripped off my blindfold and hatred filled his eyes.

I looked back to the two males and yelled, "I trusted you!"

The king slapped me hard across the face. "Silence, slave."

I spat at him in return.

He grabbed my braid, pulling my hair hard enough to make my eyes water. Death magic awoke at the edge of my senses. He threw me to the ground, pressing his shoe to my throat. He looked up to Roland. "Release his family to him."

"Father!"

I turned to see Roland crying, holding his daughter and wife. They looked between him and I, but he ushered them out.

The King looked at First Son. "You bring me a gift, so what boon can I grant?"

First Son looked like the arrogant Elf he was when I first met him. "I was told that you had a Wood Elf here. He is my rival back in our Clan." He gave the king a malicious smile. "I just want to know that he is being taken care of, so I can go back to our Clan and tell his sister that he will not be coming home, despite how hard I tried. I am sure she will reward me with everything I desire."

"You bastard! He was your friend!" I yelled at him, until the King kicked me in the stomach.

First Son just laughed. "Friend? Like I would be friends with someone so weak. But at least I have you two to thank for the Elder to believe that I was a changed Elf." He stared at the King. "You see, your Highness, she has been spreading her legs for every Wood Elf she could to stay with our Clan for as long as she had. But she has outlived her usefulness to us, so we decided that she would make a wonderful present for you." He shrugged. "Though her scars might disgust some males, she is good enough in the dark or when you want to see just how powerless she truly is while under you. How she became the so-called leader of the City Elf Rebellion is still a mystery to me."

The King laughed. "You are much different than the stories would have led us to believe, Wood Elf. I can see the viciousness and sadistic nature in your eyes, so I believe we could become good partners. I will show you where the other

Wood Elf is, then I want you to show my men where the escaped slaves went to."

"Of course." He gave the King a deep bow.

The King stood up, kicking me hard again. "Bring her along. I want those foolish slaves to see their leader before we kill her."

I saw the shock in First Son's eyes and regretfully, so did the King.

"Does her death bother you, Wood Elf?"

First Son recovered quickly. "No, your Highness. I just wonder if she is better tied to a bed as a breeder than dead. It is one thing to kill her, but another for the City Elves to see their precious leader forced to carry the child of their master."

I felt sick at the thought, but I understood what he was trying to do.

"Killing her only lasts once. Keep her as a pet, and she becomes a lifelong lesson for the City Elves to ever question their place in life."

"I like how you think, Wood Elf. And they say Wood Elves are the honorable ones."

The guards grabbed me off the ground.

"Honor only gets you so far. Ambition gets you farther."

"Right you are," the King replied as he escorted First Son and the guards carrying me down into the basement of the castle.

The air became colder as we reached the bottom of the stairs and stopped at a door, but it was not from the temperature. Everything around me felt wrong, the strong smell of death in the air. I felt the Snow Cat stirring, as she raged against my mind. She took over my body without my permission. She fought against the guard that held us.

The King slapped me, but I caught his hand in my teeth. I bit down, adding more of the scent of blood to everything. He screeched, and First Son stepped in front of me, where he hit me in the stomach hard enough for her to let him go. I hissed at him, then growled so low it was a wonder it came from my throat.

The King held his bloody hand close to his chest as the door opened. Thick congealing blood covered the floor; the smell hit us hard.

"Goddess Above!" First Son yelped as we saw the dead City Elves lining the walls.

Howling Wolf laid naked, chained in the center of the room, a woman riding him as she raped him.

There was a murderous look in the King's eyes. "Your Goddess has no place here." He grabbed me from the guards. "Hold him!"

They lunged at First Son, as other guards came through the door to make sure he would not be able to help me.

"Do you think I am a fool, Wood Elf? I knew both of my carefully cultivated Slaver Clans were destroyed by this bitch. I heard of the stories of the woman they called the Reckoning." He motioned to the dead City Elves. "Their lives showed me your campaign to free the slaves, but they also showed me where your City Elf settlement is located. Within days, my knights will capture them all, along with your Wood Elves. I just needed to get their three strongest fighters away from there. Since Roland has such a bleeding heart, I knew you would help him if he needed it. I just needed the right incentive. You almost had me fooled with your idea that I should make her a breeder." He threw me onto the ground next to his Queen as she finished with Howling Wolf.

I saw through my blue tinted vision that he was barely breathing. "What did you do to him, you bitch?" I asked the Queen.

"He needed to learn his place, so I gave him something that would make him more compliant." She gave me a smile filled with hatred, as she stroked his cheek. "How about you show our guest how good of a dog you are?"

He rolled over and faced me. There was no recognition in his eyes as he lunged at me.

I kicked him over me, as I had done many times before. He flipped over me, and I popped onto my feet. I ignored him, and I ran to the Queen, her eyes wide at the speed the Snow Cat gave me. I slid behind her from the blood covering the floor and used the chains of my shackles to wrap around her neck.

"Stay away from me, or I will kill her," I growled to the King, tightening the shackles around her throat.

"Guards! Seize her!" he told them, leaving only four near First Son.

I stayed close to the Queen's body, tightening the shackle chains as they came for us. I used her as my shield until she fell limp in my arms.

The King screamed in hatred and rage, watching the life leave his wife's eyes. "Kill her!"

I dropped the Queen's corpse onto the ground. Howling Wolf tackled me. He straddled my waist and wrapped his hands around my throat. I was unable to kick him away from me, so instead I wrapped the chains around his wrists, pulling as hard as I could to try to break them.

The Snow Car snarled and took over again. I kicked my feet up, wrapping my ankles in front of his neck, like I did with the tree during the Gauntlet. I pulled back, yanking him with it.

"Snow!" First Son called out as my daggers and sheaths slid toward me.

I untied my chains from Howling Wolf's wrists and grabbed the daggers. I then slashed at his arms, and he let go of my throat. I slashed him again, just trying to cause pain instead of harming him.

The door to the chamber opened, and Ursus burst into the room, holding his axe high. He slashed at the guards holding First Son, then the two of them tackled Howling Wolf off me.

The King tried to run, but what was left of the enslaved City Elves and Roland with his family stood there, blocking his path.

The City Elves all made signs of the Goddess of their chests. "He is yours, our Reckoning," the Patriarch of these Elves commanded. "Show him the mercy he never gave us."

"Are there any other members of the royal family who deserve execution?" I asked flatly.

Five other humans were thrown into the blood. "There is also a young daughter, but she is too young to even use the slaves, much less punish."

"The only mercy you will receive is the knowledge that your Kitten will live after today," the Snow Cat's voice reverberated off the stone walls.

The Patriarch turned to the rest of the royal family. "You stand before our Reckoning, a creature of the Goddess who will let you pay for your sins to our people. Say your prayers and take your last breaths before she lays you to rest. May the Goddess have mercy on your souls because there is none within her."

The King and three Princess drew their swords, ready to fight me. The two Princesses just stood there, the look of arrogance on their faces.

I held my two daggers. "Roland, take your family out of this place. It is not a place where your daughter should lose her childhood innocence." I then spoke to the City Elves, without taking my eyes off the royal family. "My Wolf has been poisoned with Muttsblood Weed. Can you get rid of the effects?"

"Yes, Reckoning," the Patriarch answered. A few of the City Elves escorted Roland and his family from the chamber, while others went to help hold Howling Wolf down, with even more rushing the antidote.

"Once we kill you, we will hunt down every last Elf and destroy them until nothing is left of your race except stories," one of the Princesses yelled.

I waited until the City Elves gave Howling Wolf the antidote to the Muttsblood Weed, and he screamed in pain.

"Then cut me down, if you can." The Snow Cat and I were one, our movements fluid as we gave them their death dance. We moved with their movements, dodging their swords, slashing at them with cuts that hurt and bled, but we did not kill. The Princesses watched with wide eyes as I sliced their males to pieces. I disemboweled them, just as I did Viper, before reaching the women. They begged for their lives, but I slashed their throats open, letting them fall to the floor.

The Necromantic circle activated with their deaths and blood. "Goddess Above!" someone whispered. The spirits of the fallen City Elves rose to their feet. They walked over to their friends, saying their last goodbyes, while they passed by me, thanking me for being their Reckoning.

The Snow Cat's spirit howled as her blue spirit pulled away from me. I saw the small spirits of her Kittens running to her, as well as a larger male.

I knelt. "Thank you for everything. I would not have survived without you. Enjoy your afterlife with your family." I smiled to Howling Wolf, First Son, and Ursus. I saw pride in their eyes, and something else in Howling Wolf's. "I finally found mine."

She purred against me then I felt her leave, her blue spirit nuzzling against her mate and her Kittens batting at her. My body became weaker, the Snow Cat's energy no longer strengthening my own. Darkness closed around me, as I fell.

Chapter 27

"Snow? Are you awake? We are almost to the settlement," someone whispered to me.

I opened my eyes and saw First Son sitting there next to me in the covered wagon.

"How long?" My voice was rough.

"For about a week. We made Roland's family into the new royal line, under threat of returning to finish the job against the humans if they tried to disagree. King Roland's first duty was to completely abolish the slave trade, and then he got to work making the kingdom better. We have been travelling for five days, and we were not sure when you were going to wake up."

I closed my eyes but stayed awake. "Ah. Please do not tell Sparrow or the Matriarch that I played bait. I enjoy having a pillow when I sleep."

"You have a pillow at Wolf's house."

"But—" I started to remind him about Doe when we heard voices outside of the wagon.

"It is Ursus and Wolf!" the Kitten yelled from outside. "Where is Snow?"

"Back here, Kitten!" I shouted as First Son helped me sit up.

The covered part of the wagon ripped away, and the boy climbed into the back. "Is Snow all right?" He hugged me.

"Yes, Kitten." I hugged him back, before giving him a grin. "Did you hug Sparrow?"

"And he punched the Matriarch." Sparrow grinned as she helped me out of the wagon.

"Good, Kitten." I snuggled him, then set him back on the ground. I stretched, as First Son grabbed Sparrow and lifted him into his arms.

Ursus grabbed Cristata, and Doe popped out of the building she was in. She ran toward Howling Wolf, leaping into his arms, and I ran the opposite way to the bathhouse.

The Matriarch came in after me. "Welcome home, Snow."

I stripped from my bloody clothes and dove into the water. I came back up, feeling better. "We could not save them all, Matriarch. The King used some of them for a Necromantic ritual. Your ally, Roland, is the new King and has already abolished slavery."

She climbed into the pool with me and leaned against the side. "We knew that not everyone would survive, Snow. But the important thing is that we were able to get our people to freedom."

"You are right, Matriarch. We also need to decide what we are going to do next. Are we going to let the Clans go back to how they were separated before, just with new additions, or are we going to create our own cities?"

"Have you heard of Ironheart Trees?" she asked me.

I shook my head. "No."

"Ironheart Trees are ones that have the ability for homes to be created in them. The Moon Clan's Grandfather was telling me about them, and how the Wood Elves used to live in them before they built villages. I was thinking that maybe we should find these Trees as stopover places between the Clan villages," She explained.

"Maybe we should withdraw from the cities completely. We have our people, so maybe it would be worth just dealing with other Elves. Let the humans have their cold stone buildings, while we get the warmth of our wooden homes."

"Do you not mean trees, since you have the Snow Cat?"

I shook my head. "I promised her that after we liberated our people, we would find a way to set her free. The Necromancy took care of that for us, and she passed into the underworld."

"May she rest with the Goddess and Her Dark Consort." She gave a small prayer.

"She has her kittens and her mate, so she will be fine."

She flipped over, so she was facing the edge of the pool. "What about you?"

"What about me?"

"You and Howling Wolf."

"There is nothing to say about it. Did you not see Doe leap into his arms?"

"But you did not see that I turned her away when she tried to kiss me." Howling Wolf's voice rumbled through the bathhouse.

"On that note, I think I am clean enough for dinner." The Matriarch smiled and got out of the pool, grabbed her clothes, then left the area.

I flipped around and stared at him. "What do you mean? You still love her."

He sat next to me, dipping his feet and legs into the pool. "You have it wrong, Snow. I was angry at her getting sold into slavery, because she is not as strong as you are, and I knew they would use her the way you have been used. When I was talking to her son, I remembered that I loved her once, but when I saw you coming back with the ledger, the only thing I could think of was wanting to have a child with you. I am sorry that it came across wrong. I wanted to explain it to you, but you practically ran from me. Snow, I loved Doe a long time ago, but she is not the one I want to spend my life with." He grabbed me and sat me in his lap. "I want to spend it with you. Not just as my Second, but as my partner."

I touched some of the new scars on his back. "I am sorry for everything you went through, Howling Wolf. I was so distraught and trapped in my own jealousy, that I could not see out of it. Because of that, you spent a year as a slave, when you could have been free." I lifted his wrist and looked at his brand. "Because I refused to talk with you, you have something I would have ever wished on anyone. Because I am an idiot, you were given Muttsblood Weed and raped."

He held me close. "I could have stopped you and explained everything, but I did not. It is on both of us for not communicating. We are together now, so I will ask you again. Will you become official with me, stand with me in front of the Clan to pronounce our intent to be partners for life?"

"I will ask you for the last time: are you sure you want me?"

"There was never a doubt in my mind, Snow."

"Then yes."

He leaned his face forward, and we kissed each other softly, before it became a greater need to feel each other. I grinned and pulled away. Then I wrapped my arms around his neck, leaning back with all my weight.

"Wolf? Snow?" Sparrow asked as I pulled us into the pool of water, splashing the sides of the edge. She laughed when she saw the drenched Howling Wolf. "Took you two long enough to get everything figured out."

I splashed water at her, but she left us alone. "I accept you as my partner, for as long as I live. I wish for us to have the best lives together, taking on every challenge we face. Through peace and war, good times and bad, you are the only one I want to spend the rest of my days with," I told him, then kissed him again.

About The Author Sarah Thomie

My name is S. Thomie (pronounced 'Tommy'). I was born and raised in Las Vegas, then moved to North Carolina, until I somehow ended up in Oklahoma for College. I have worked retail, food service, as a map maker, in the military, as a driver, in a Magic Shop, as a government contractor, and in a factory that makes synthetic thread. Now, my goal is to write full time as a professionally published Author.

At home, I have a husband, two daughters, and two cats (a black cat, Asha, and an orange cat, Cali).